S0-BZF-942

J.M. BARRIE'S

PETER PAN

A GRAPHIC NOVEL

BY BLAKE HOENA
& FERNANDO CANO

STONE ARCH BOOKS
A CAPSTONE IMPRINT

Graphic Revolve is published by Stone Arch Books
A Capstone Imprint
1710 Roe Crest Drive, North Mankato, Minnesota 56003
www.capstonepub.com

Cataloging-in-Publication Data is available at the Library
of Congress website.
Hardcover ISBN: 978-1-4965-0372-5
Paperback ISBN: 978-1-4965-0380-0
Ebook PDF ISBN: 978-1-4965-2318-1

Summary: Peter Pan is a special boy. He can fly. He
doesn't grow old. And he comes from a magical island
called Neverland. So when Peter shows up at the Darling
residence, Wendy and her brothers are all too eager
to follow Peter on the adventure of a lifetime. But the
Darlings find themselves caught in the middle of a battle
between Peter's gang of orphans, the Lost Boys, and a
band of pirates led by the treacherous Captain Hook. Will
Peter be able to protect the Darlings while leading the
Lost Boys to victory? Or will Captain Hook make Peter
Pan walk the plank?

Common Core back matter written by Dr. Katie Monnin

Designer: Bob Lentz

Printed in the United States of America in Stevens Point,
Wisconsin.
052015   008824WZ15

TABLE OF CONTENTS

ALL ABOUT PETER PAN

Scottish writer J.M. Barrie first had his character Peter Pan appear in his adult novel *The Little White Bird* in 1902. However, the character's most popular appearance came in late 1904 in the stage play *Peter Pan, or The Boy Who Wouldn't Grow Up*. The play's version of the character turned out to be so popular that J.M Barrie published the novel *Peter and Wendy* in 1911 as a sort of novelized version of the play. Ever since, the character has appeared in movies, television shows, other plays, and even animated cartoons.

Because J.M. Barrie didn't provide many details about Peter Pan's appearance, adaptations of the character have shown him in a wide variety of ways. When played on stage, the role of Peter Pan is usually played by an adult woman!

Peter Pan's costume has changed many times over the years, including everything from a red tunic with green leggings to a green costume made of leaves. Most often the character has red hair and blue (or green) eyes. In the Disney film, Peter Pan wears a feathered cap and a green tunic.

In the original play, Peter insists that no one can ever touch him, and the stage directions for the play itself indicate that other characters shouldn't make physical contact with Peter. In one scene, Wendy tries to give Peter a kiss, but Tinker Bell puts a stop to it. It is never explained why Peter shouldn't be touched. Recent adaptations of the play have often ignored this aspect of the tale.

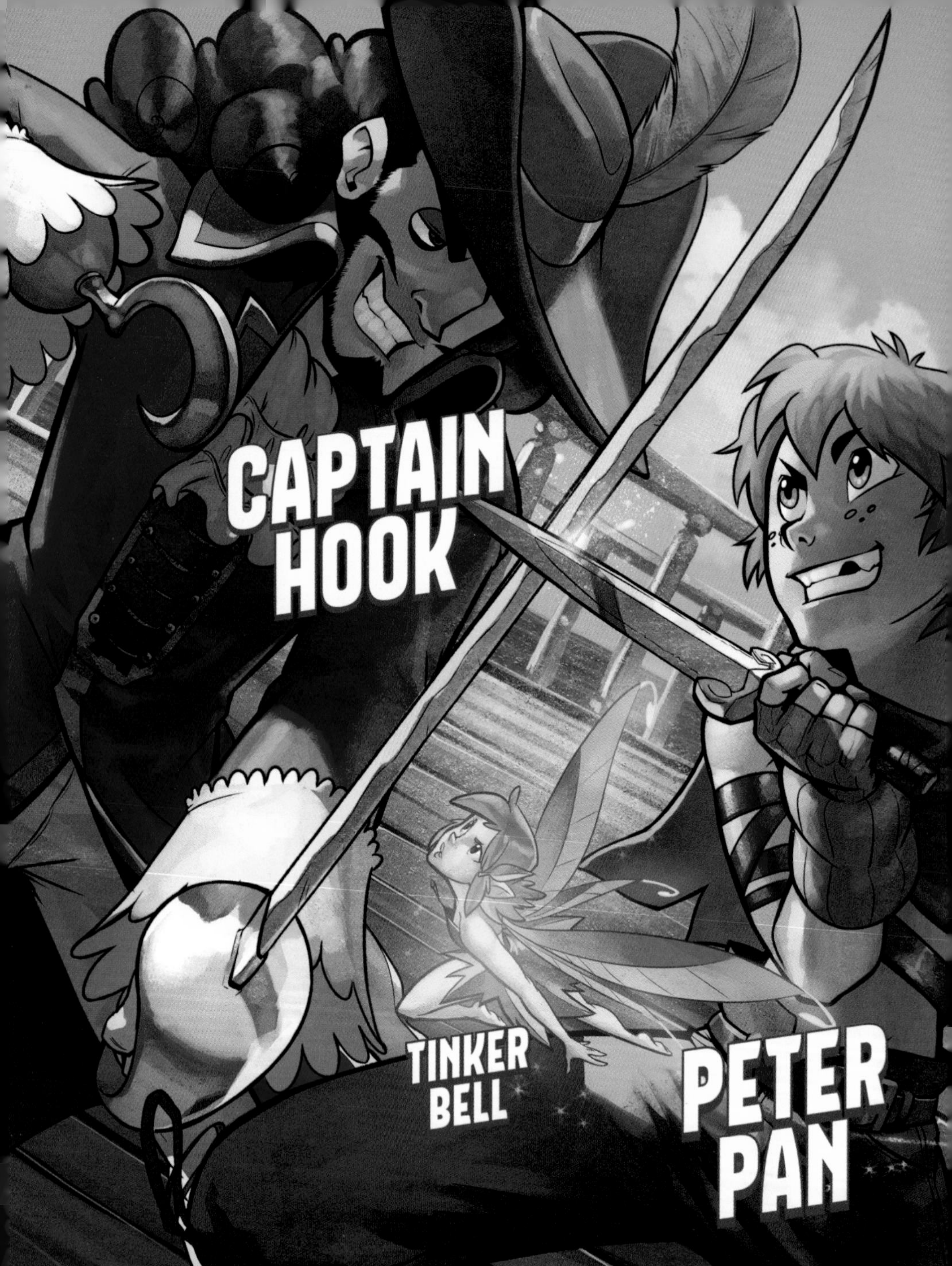
CAPTAIN HOOK
TINKER BELL
PETER PAN

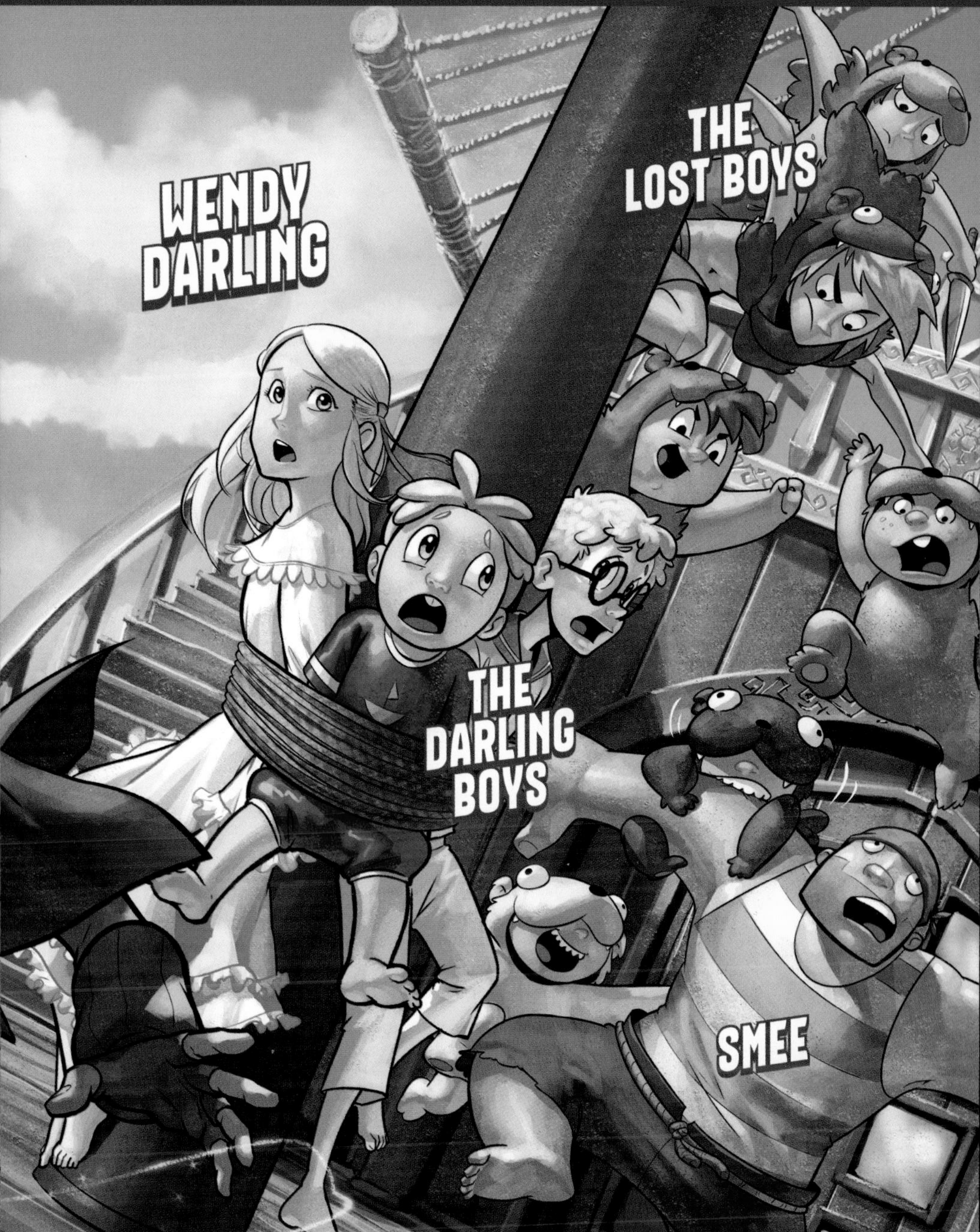
WENDY DARLING
THE LOST BOYS
THE DARLING BOYS
SMEE

CHAPTER 1
THE SHADOW

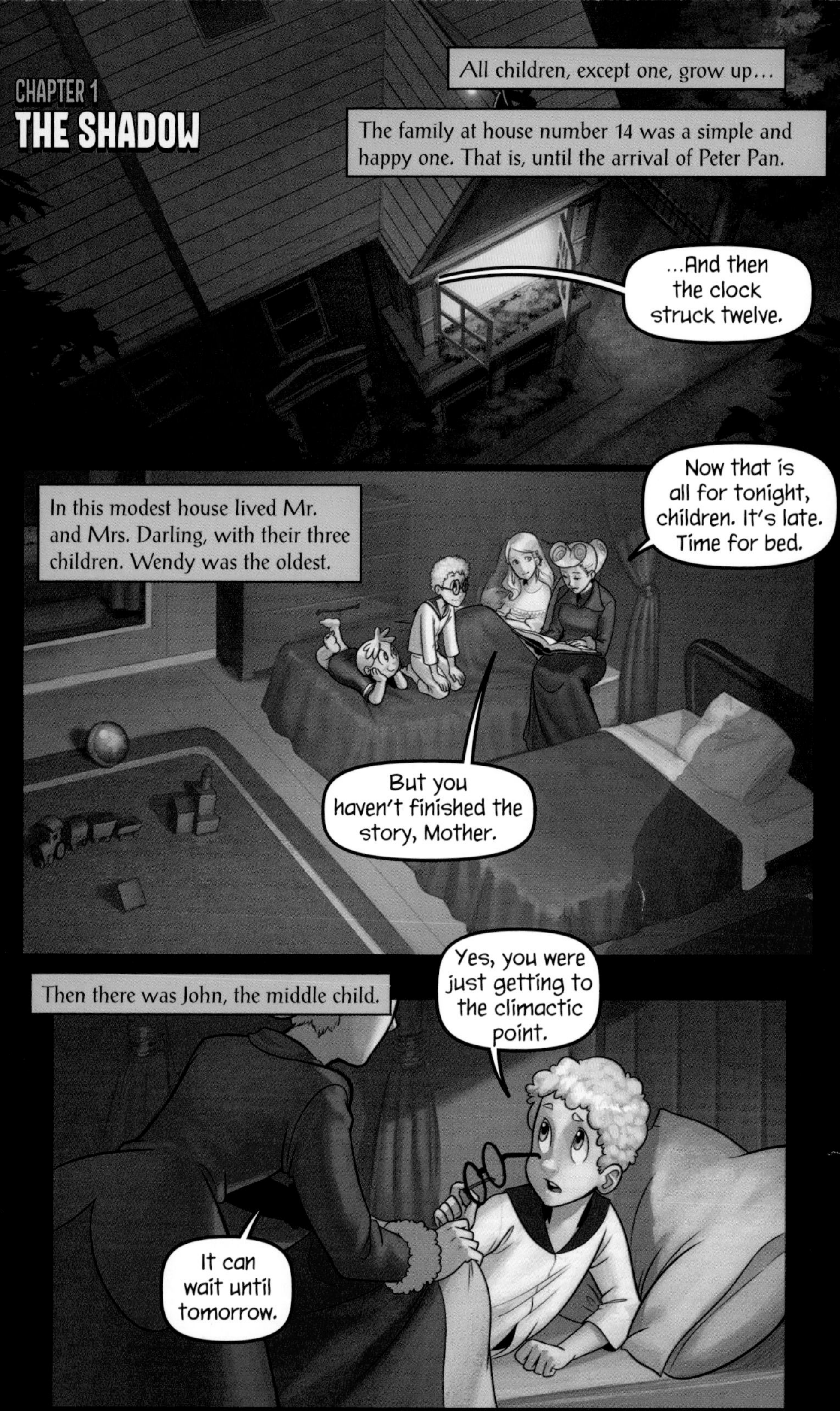
All children, except one, grow up...
The family at house number 14 was a simple and happy one. That is, until the arrival of Peter Pan.
...And then the clock struck twelve.
In this modest house lived Mr. and Mrs. Darling, with their three children. Wendy was the oldest.
Now that is all for tonight, children. It's late. Time for bed.
But you haven't finished the story, Mother.
Then there was John, the middle child.
Yes, you were just getting to the climactic point.
It can wait until tomorrow.

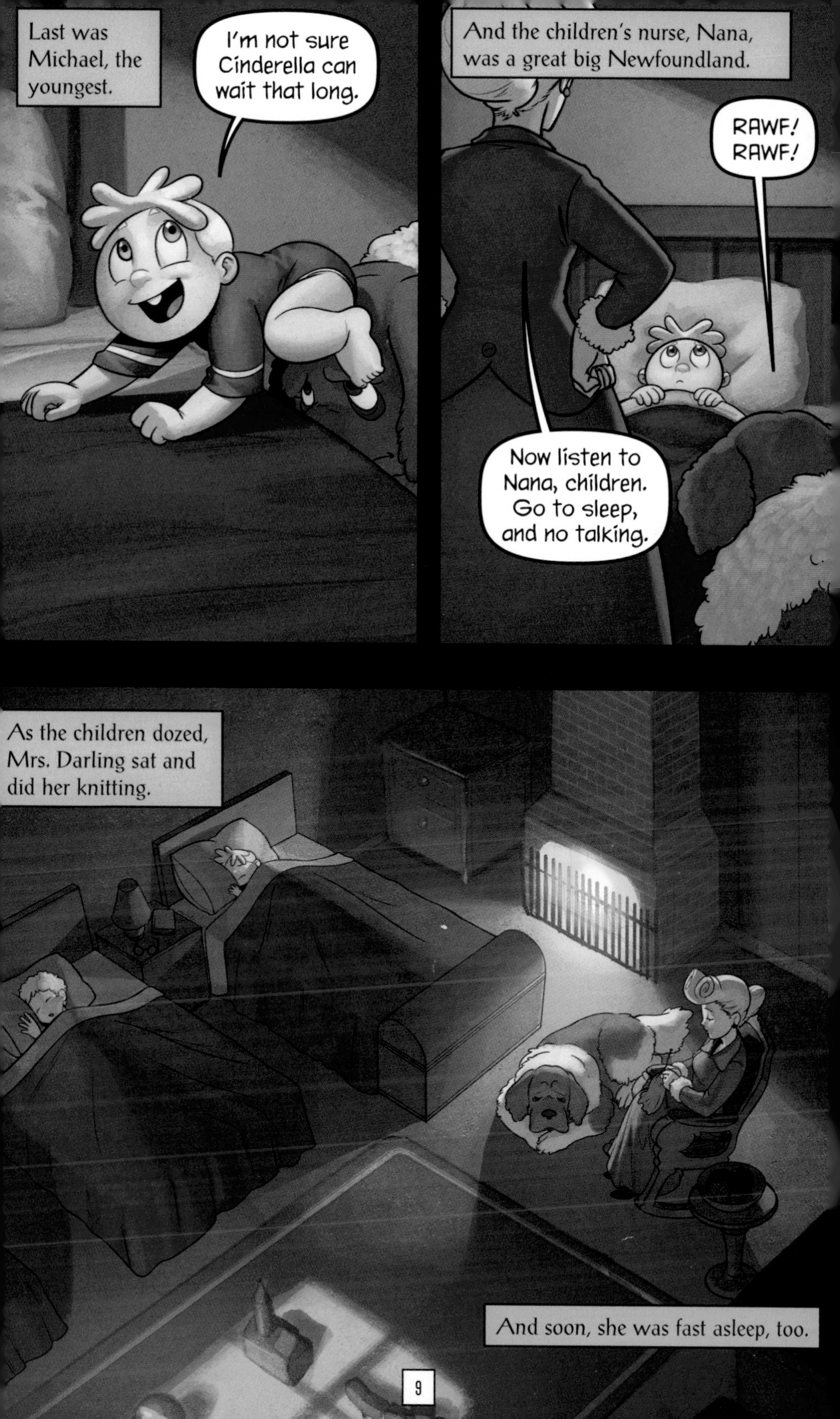
Last was Michael, the youngest.
I'm not sure Cinderella can wait that long.
And the children's nurse, Nana, was a great big Newfoundland.
RAWF! RAWF!
Now listen to Nana, children. Go to sleep, and no talking.
As the children dozed, Mrs. Darling sat and did her knitting.
And soon, she was fast asleep, too.

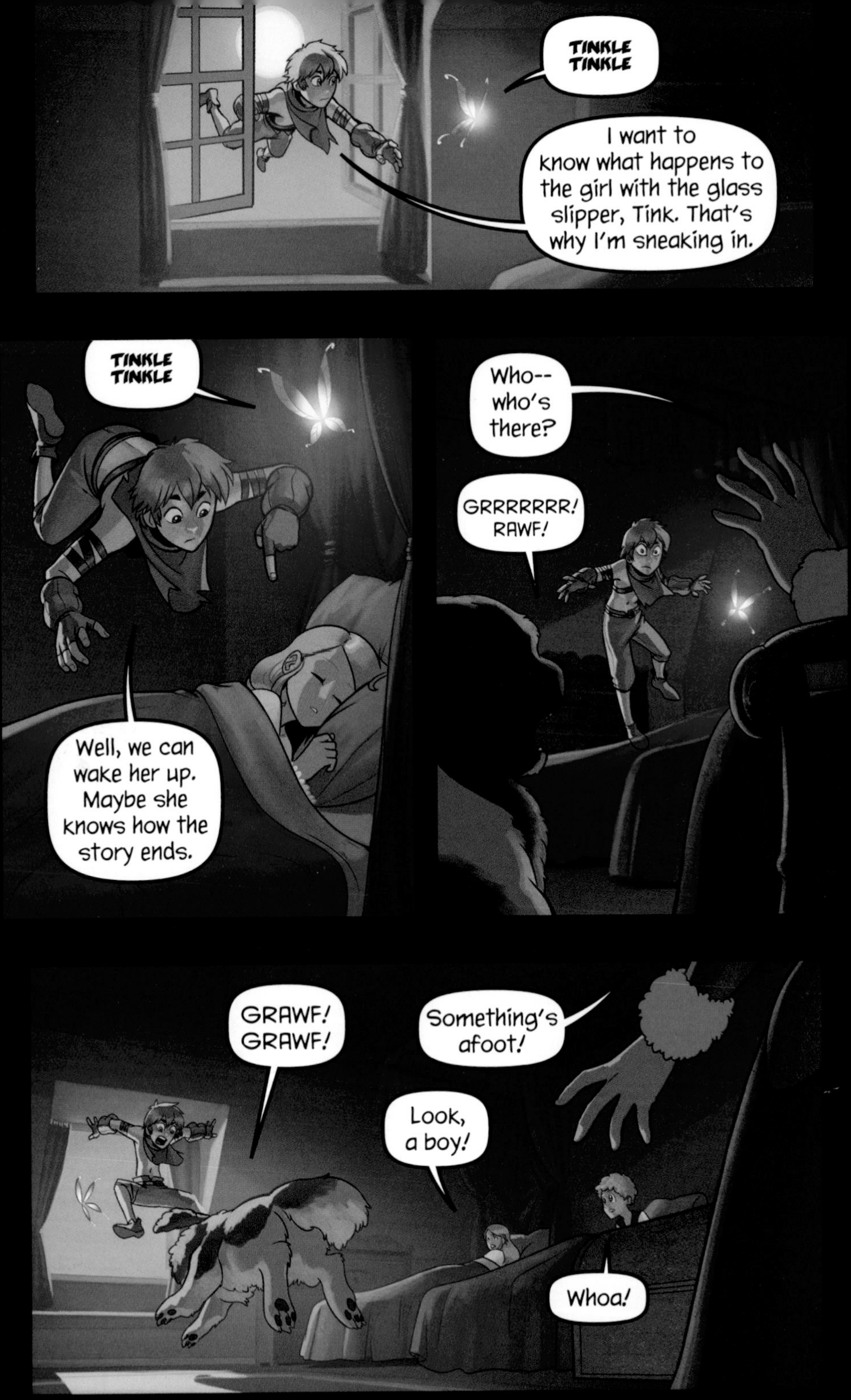
TINKLE TINKLE
I want to know what happens to the girl with the glass slipper, Tink. That's why I'm sneaking in.
TINKLE TINKLE
Well, we can wake her up. Maybe she knows how the story ends.
Who-- who's there?
GRRRRRRR! RAWF!
GRAWF! GRAWF!
Something's afoot!
Look, a boy!
Whoa!

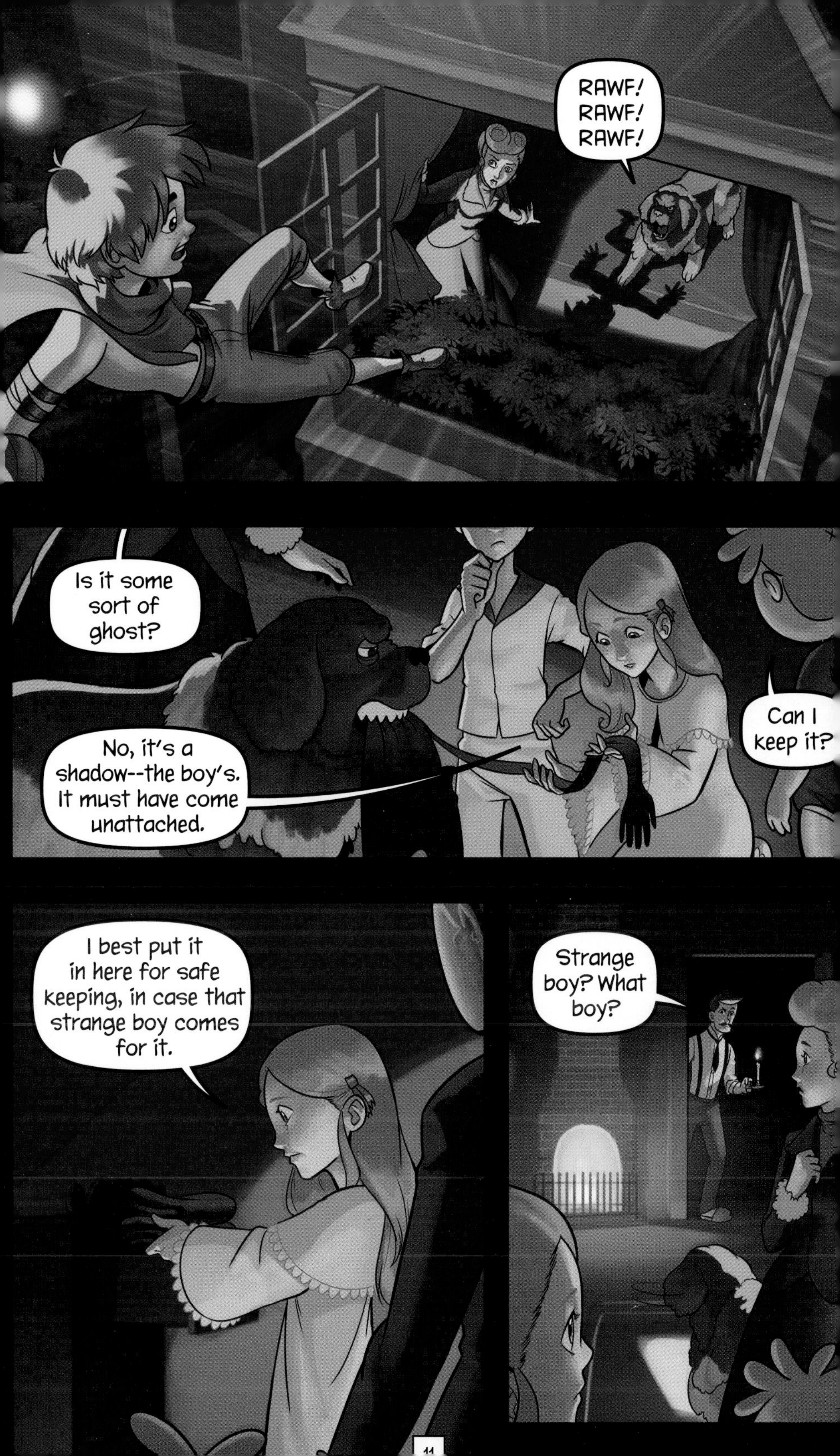
RAWF! RAWF! RAWF!
Is it some sort of ghost?
No, it's a shadow--the boy's. It must have come unattached.
Can I keep it?
I best put it in here for safe keeping, in case that strange boy comes for it.
Strange boy? What boy?

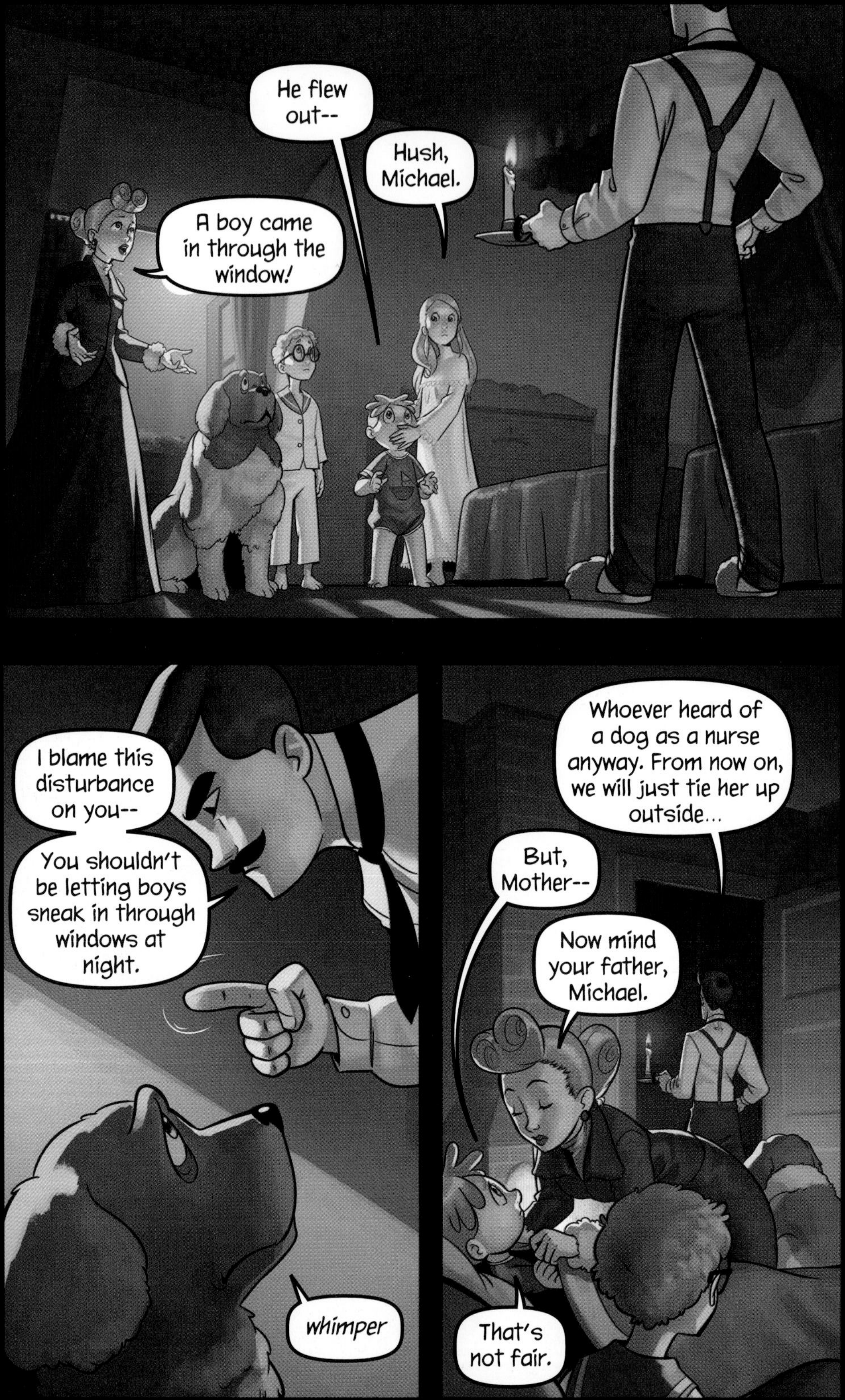
A boy came in through the window!
He flew out--
Hush, Michael.
I blame this disturbance on you--
You shouldn't be letting boys sneak in through windows at night.
whimper
Whoever heard of a dog as a nurse anyway. From now on, we will just tie her up outside...
But, Mother--
Now mind your father, Michael.
That's not fair.

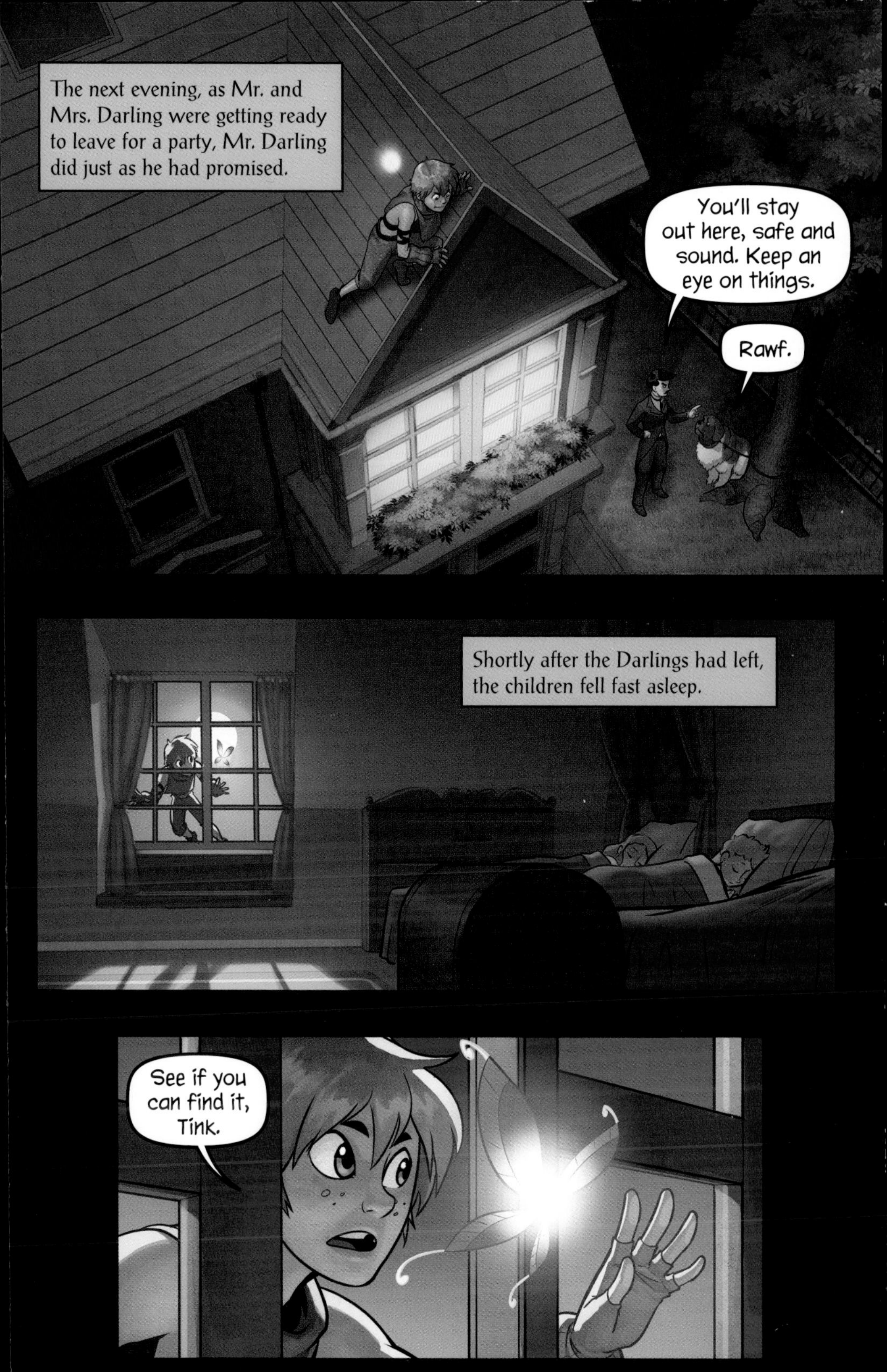
The next evening, as Mr. and Mrs. Darling were getting ready to leave for a party, Mr. Darling did just as he had promised.
You'll stay out here, safe and sound. Keep an eye on things.
Rawf.
Shortly after the Darlings had left, the children fell fast asleep.
See if you can find it, Tink.

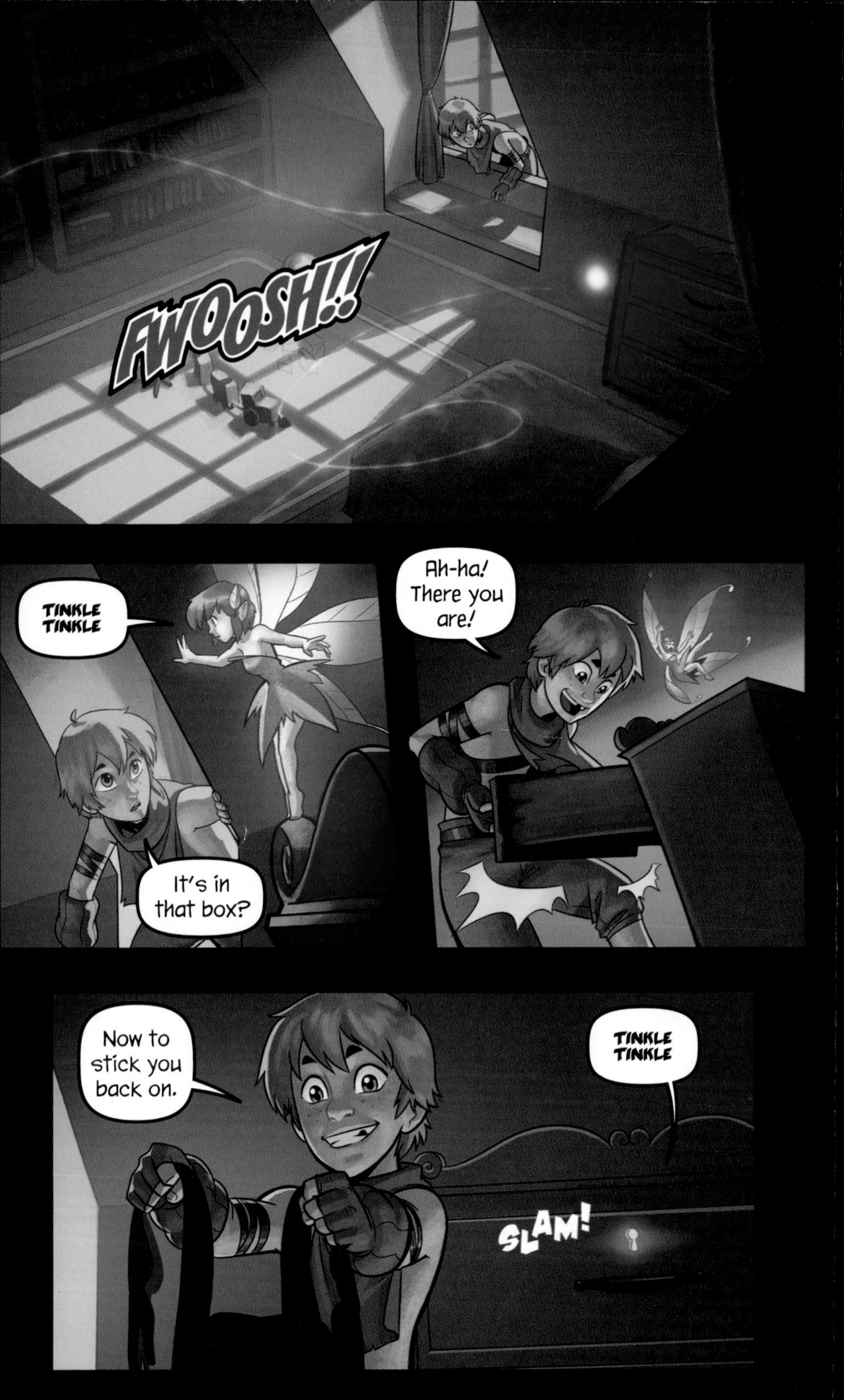
FWOOSH!!
TINKLE TINKLE
It's in that box?
Ah-ha! There you are!
Now to stick you back on.
TINKLE TINKLE
SLAM!

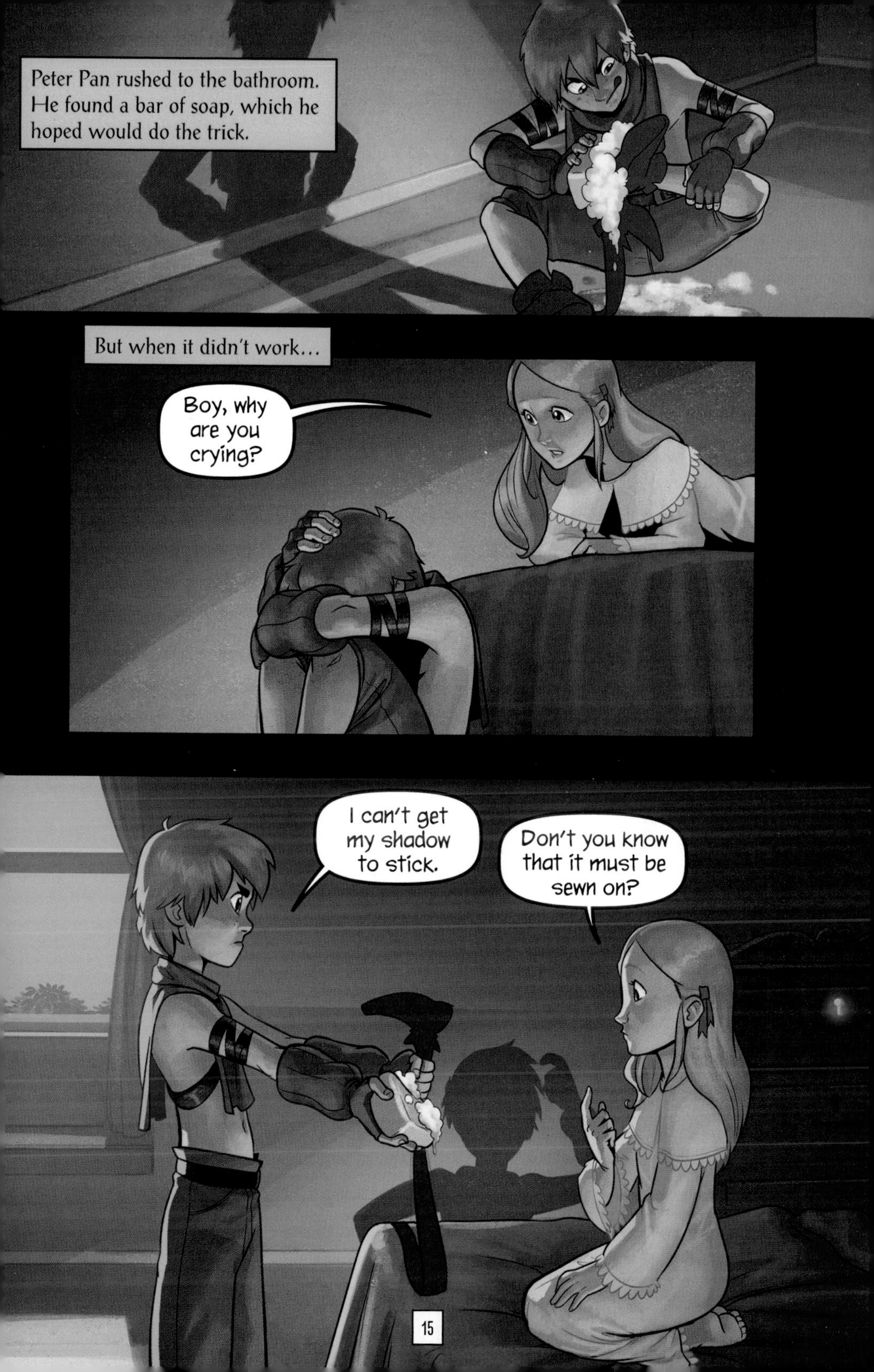
Peter Pan rushed to the bathroom. He found a bar of soap, which he hoped would do the trick.
But when it didn't work...
Boy, why are you crying?
I can't get my shadow to stick.
Don't you know that it must be sewn on?

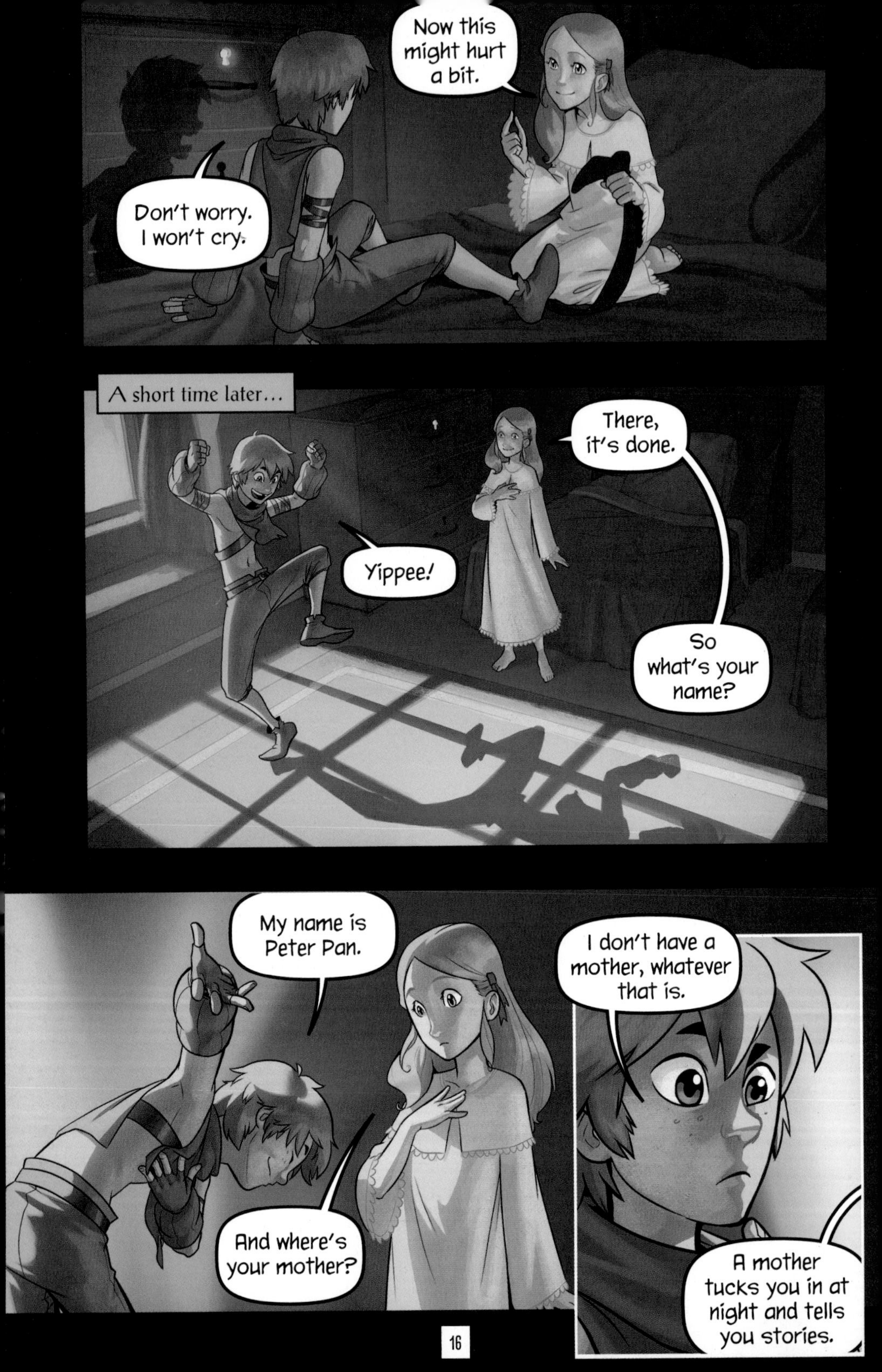
Now this might hurt a bit.
Don't worry. I won't cry.
A short time later…
There, it's done.
Yippee!
So what's your name?
My name is Peter Pan.
And where's your mother?
I don't have a mother, whatever that is.
A mother tucks you in at night and tells you stories.

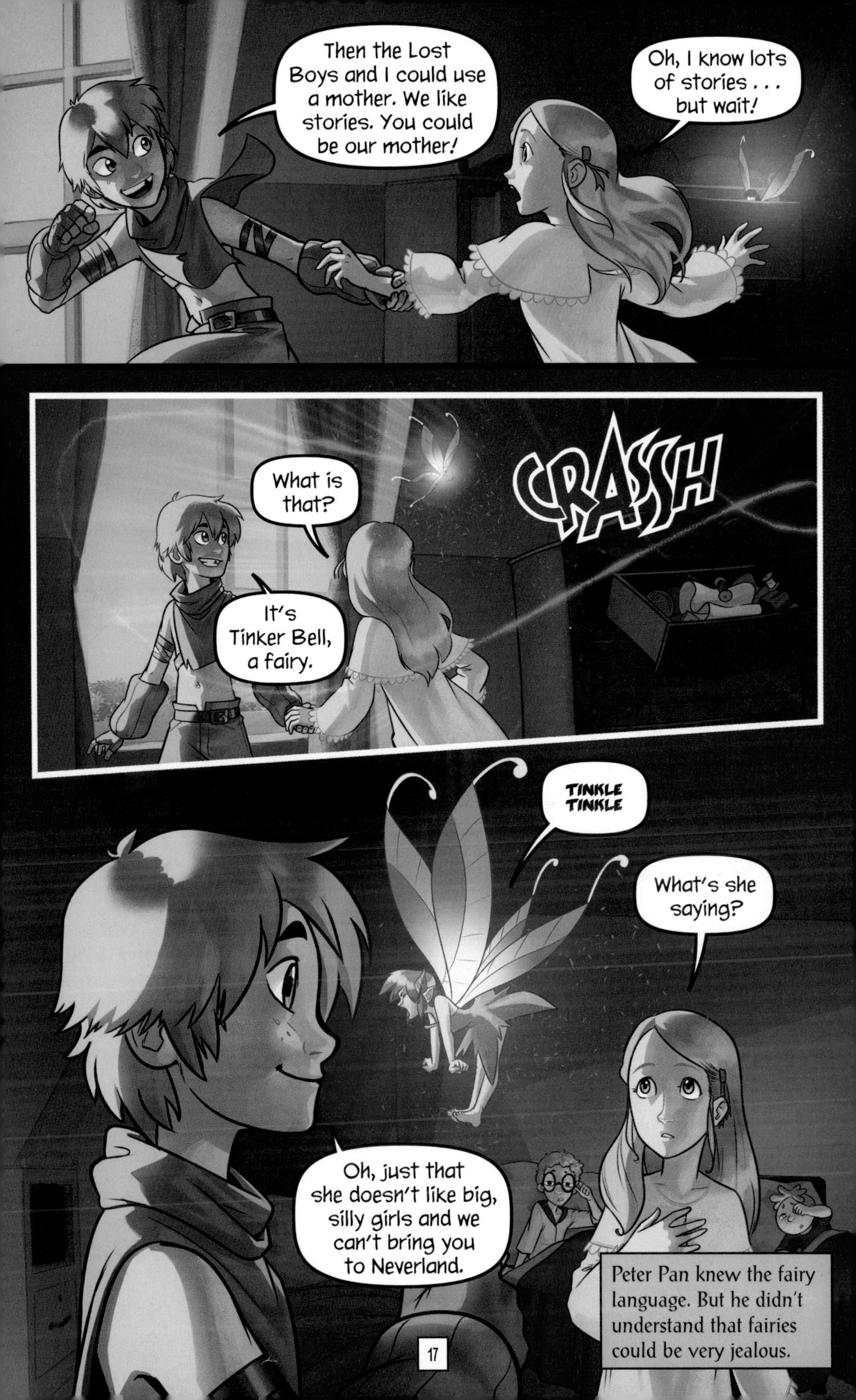
Then the Lost Boys and I could use a mother. We like stories. You could be our mother!
Oh, I know lots of stories . . . but wait!
What is that?
CRASH
It's Tinker Bell, a fairy.
TINKLE TINKLE
What's she saying?
Oh, just that she doesn't like big, silly girls and we can't bring you to Neverland.
Peter Pan knew the fairy language. But he didn't understand that fairies could be very jealous.

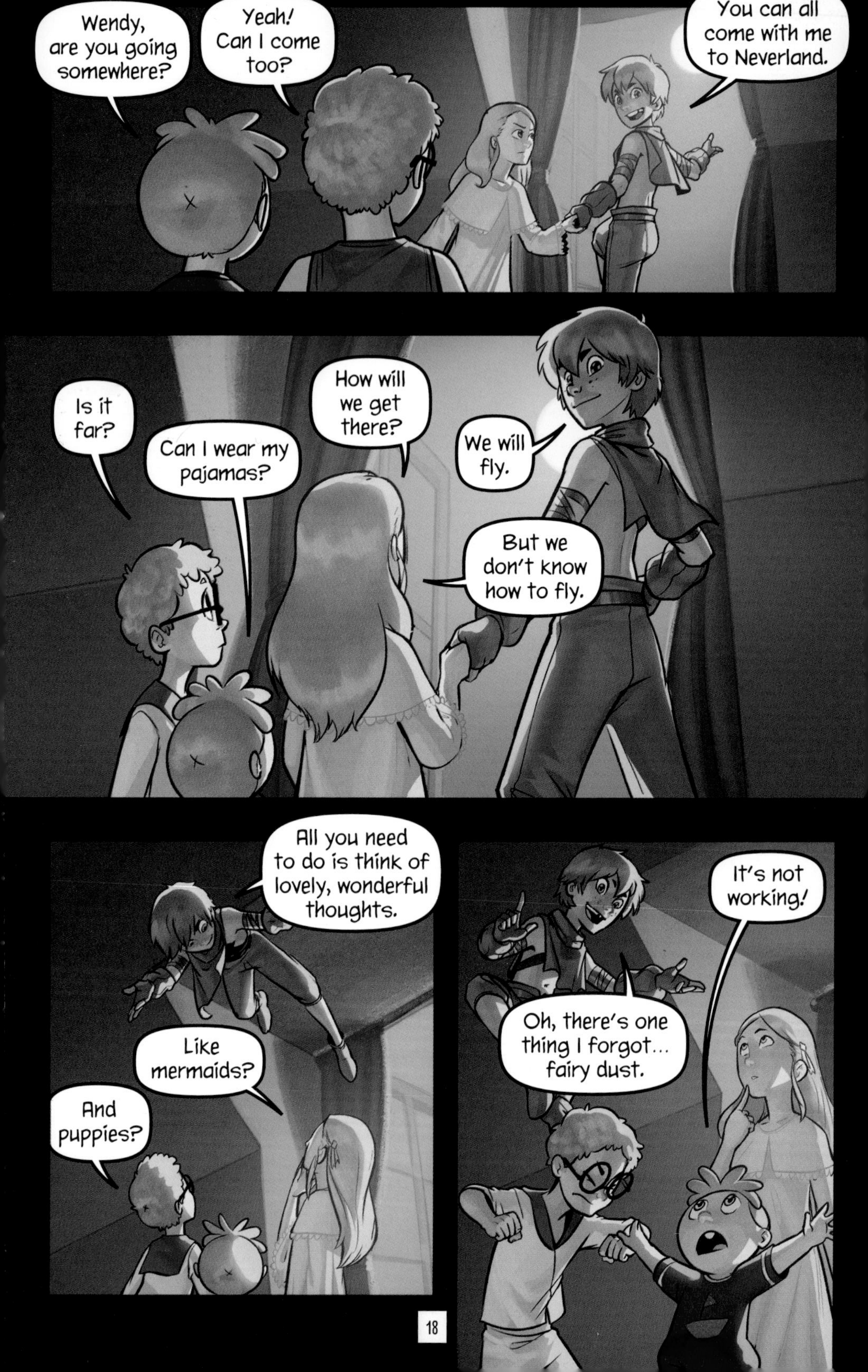

Wendy, are you going somewhere?
Yeah! Can I come too?
You can all come with me to Neverland.
Is it far?
Can I wear my pajamas?
How will we get there?
We will fly.
But we don't know how to fly.
All you need to do is think of lovely, wonderful thoughts.
Like mermaids?
And puppies?
It's not working!
Oh, there's one thing I forgot... fairy dust.

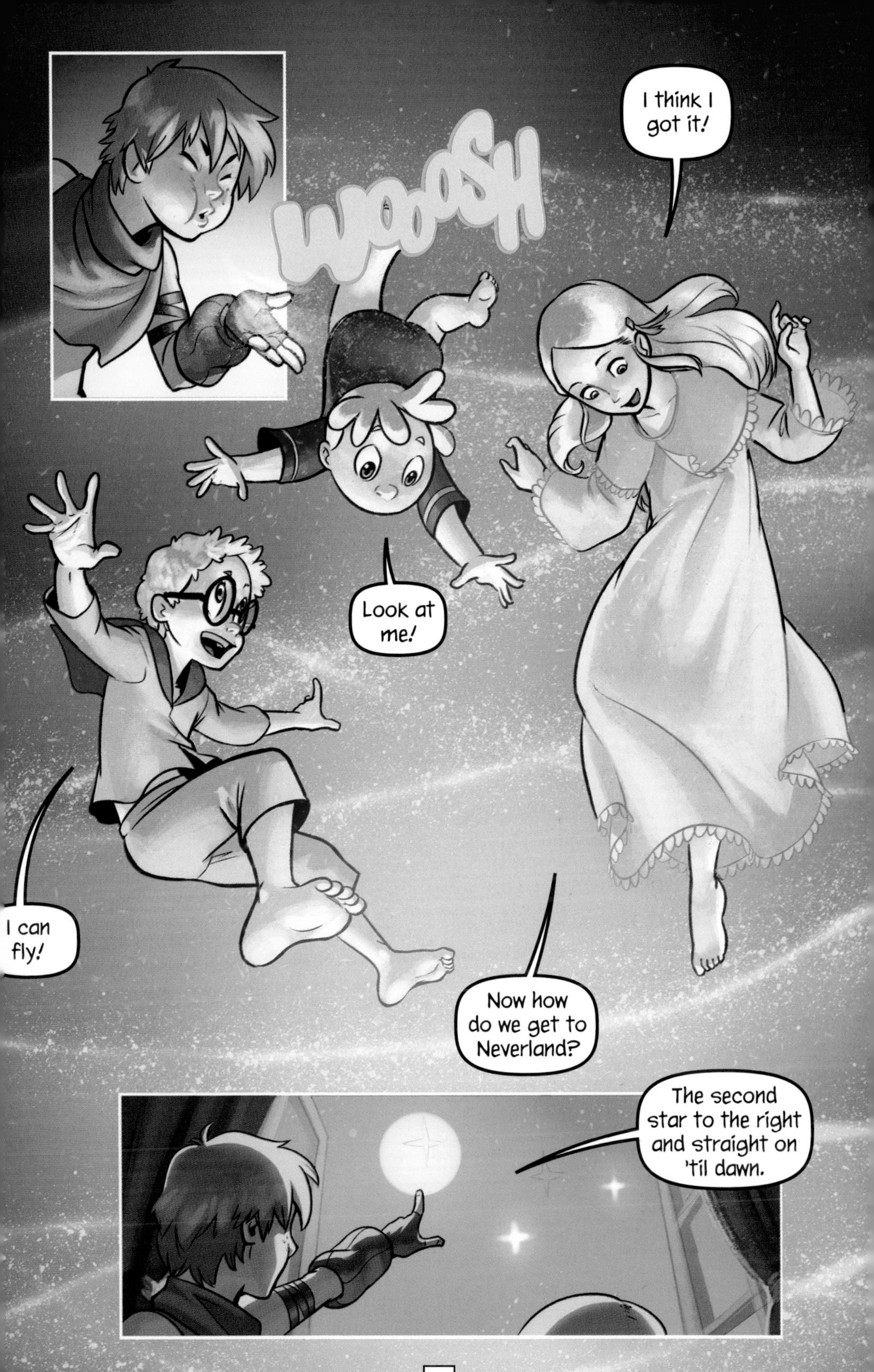
WOOOSH
I think I got it!
Look at me!
I can fly!
Now how do we get to Neverland?
The second star to the right and straight on 'til dawn.

CHAPTER 2
NEVERLAND

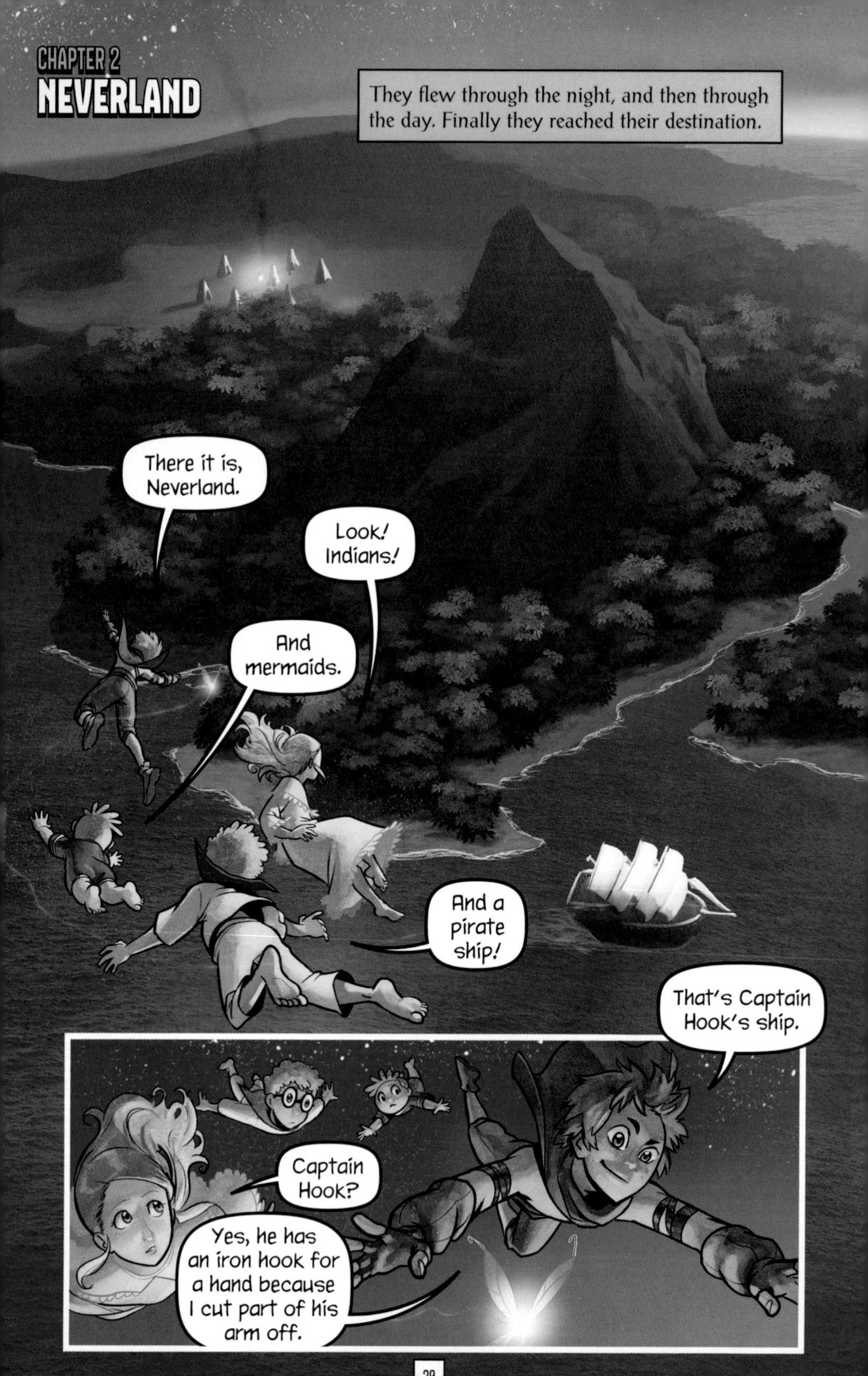

They flew through the night, and then through the day. Finally they reached their destination.
There it is, Neverland.
Look! Indians!
And mermaids.
And a pirate ship!
That's Captain Hook's ship.
Captain Hook?
Yes, he has an iron hook for a hand because I cut part of his arm off.

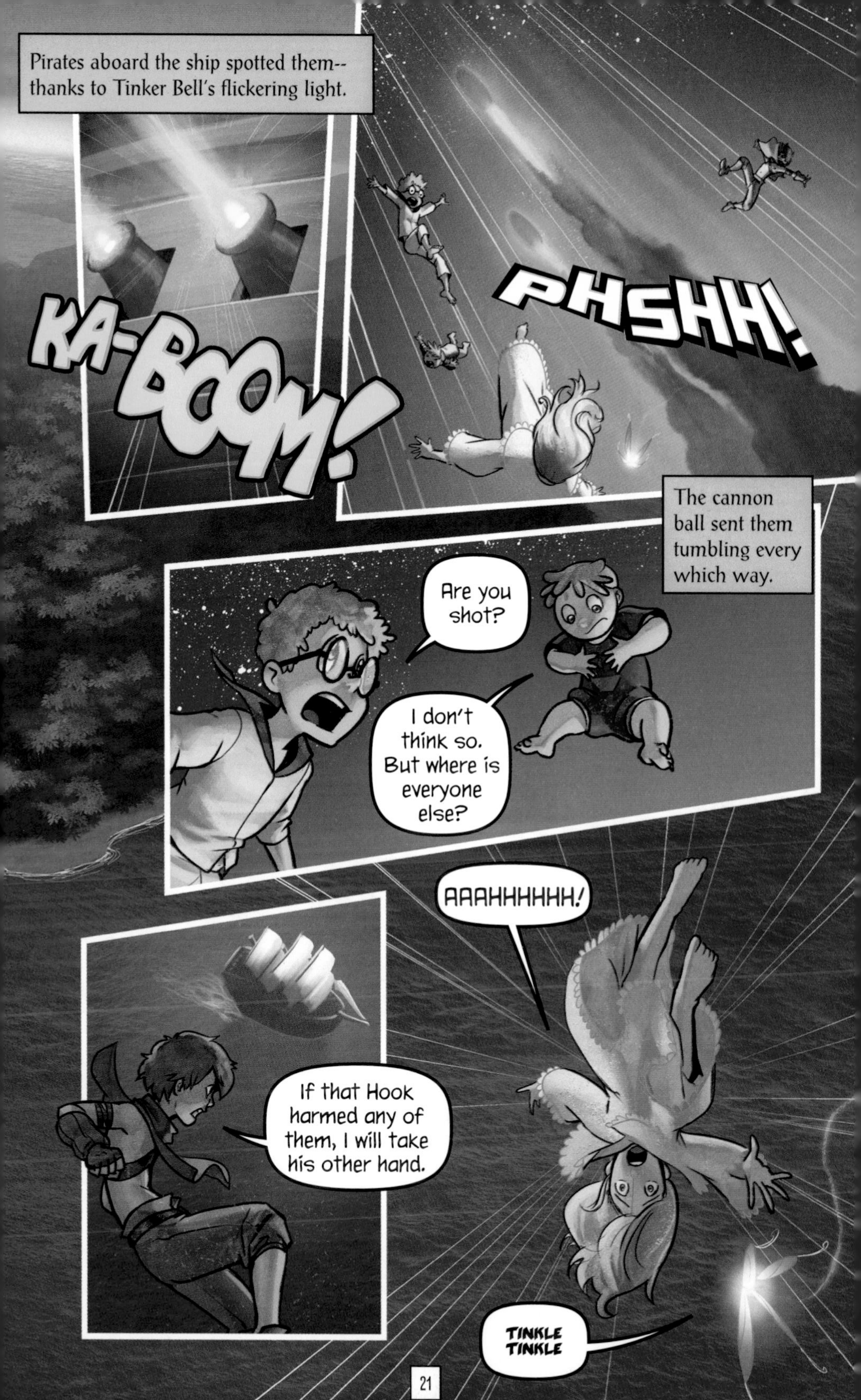

Pirates aboard the ship spotted them--thanks to Tinker Bell's flickering light.
KA-BOOM!
PHSHH!
The cannon ball sent them tumbling every which way.
Are you shot?
I don't think so. But where is everyone else?
AAAHHHHHH!
If that Hook harmed any of them, I will take his other hand.
TINKLE TINKLE

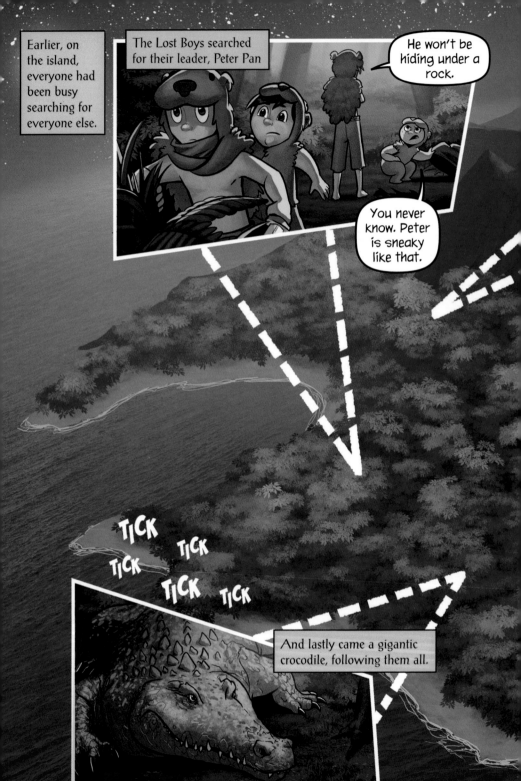

Earlier, on the island, everyone had been busy searching for everyone else.

The Lost Boys searched for their leader, Peter Pan

He won't be hiding under a rock.

You never know. Peter is sneaky like that.

TICK TICK TICK TICK TICK

And lastly came a gigantic crocodile, following them all.

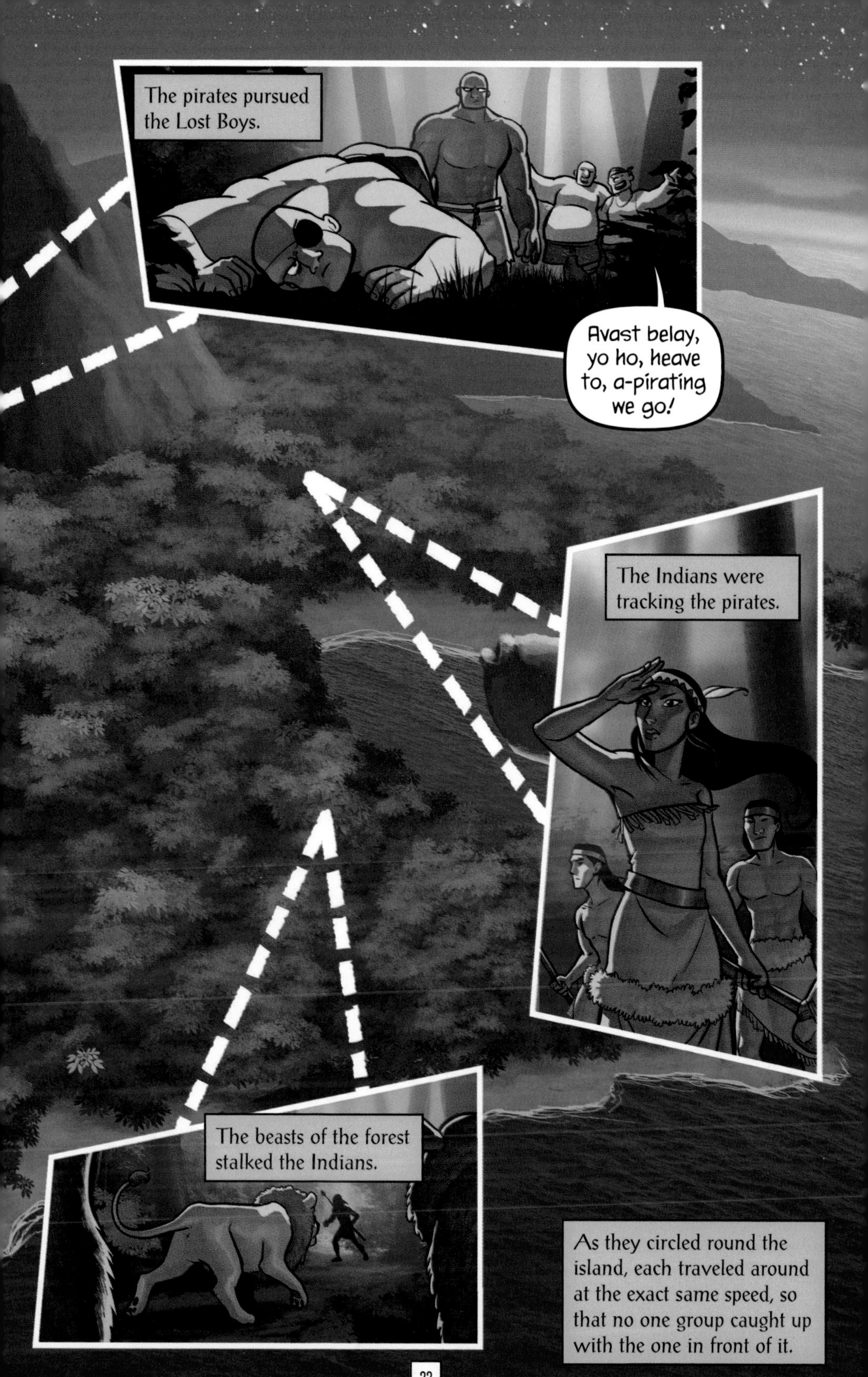
The pirates pursued the Lost Boys.
Avast belay, yo ho, heave to, a-pirating we go!
The Indians were tracking the pirates.
The beasts of the forest stalked the Indians.
As they circled round the island, each traveled around at the exact same speed, so that no one group caught up with the one in front of it.

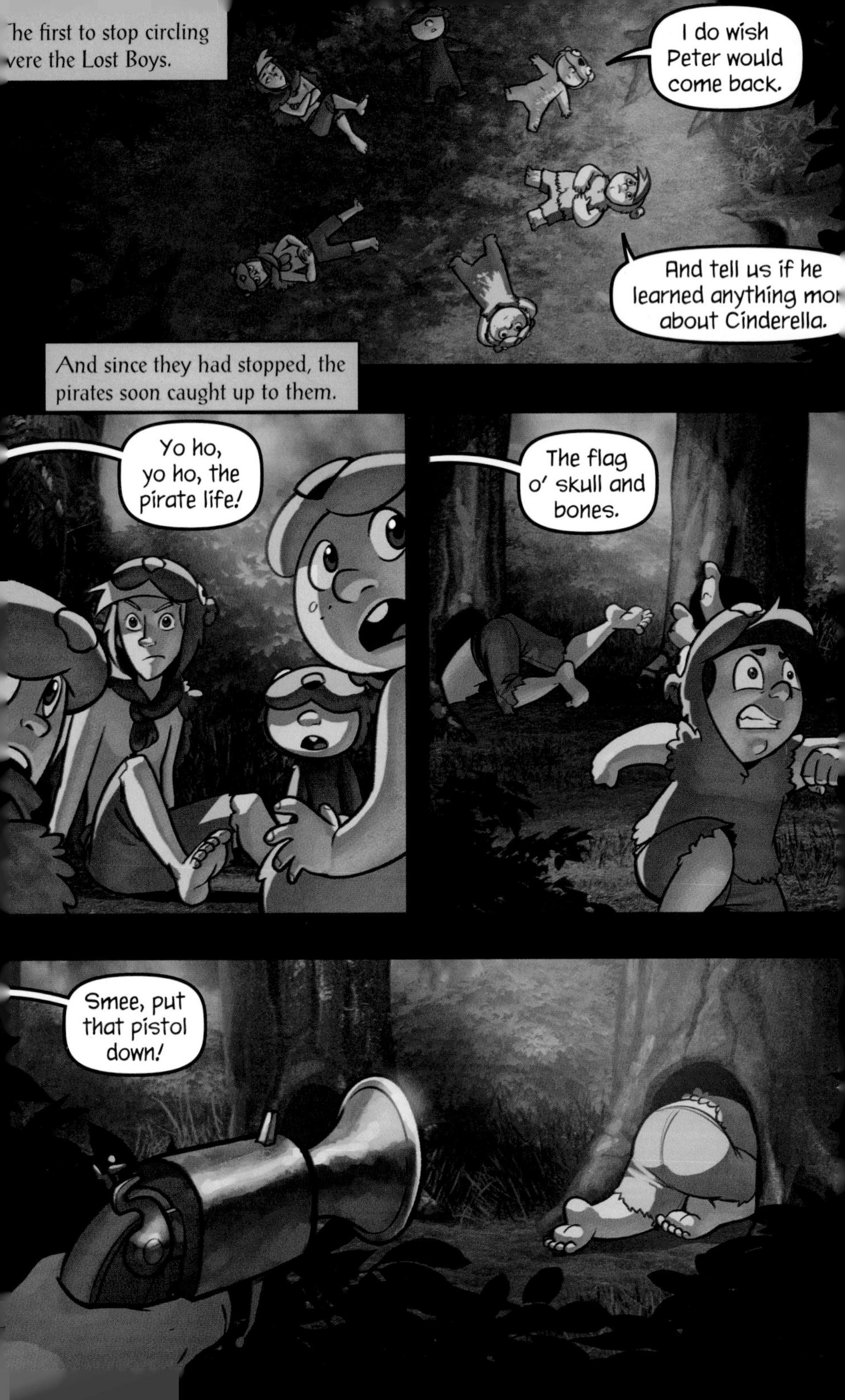
he first to stop circling
vere the Lost Boys.
I do wish Peter would come back.
And tell us if he learned anything mor about Cinderella.
And since they had stopped, the pirates soon caught up to them.
Yo ho, yo ho, the pirate life!
The flag o' skull and bones.
Smee, put that pistol down!

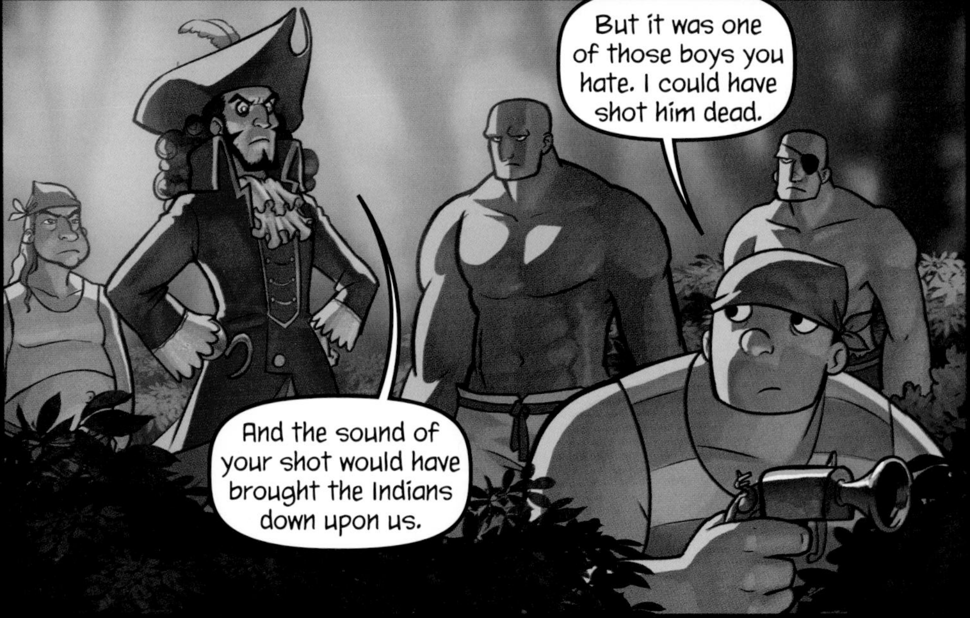
But it was one of those boys you hate. I could have shot him dead.
And the sound of your shot would have brought the Indians down upon us.

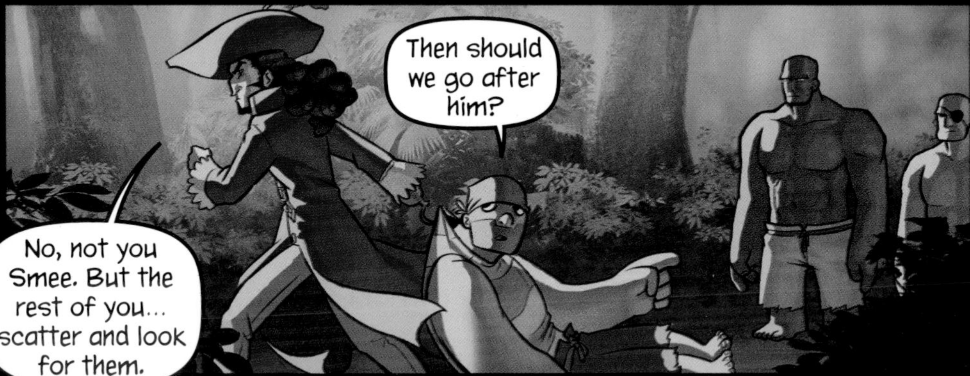
Then should we go after him?
No, not you Smee. But the rest of you... scatter and look for them.

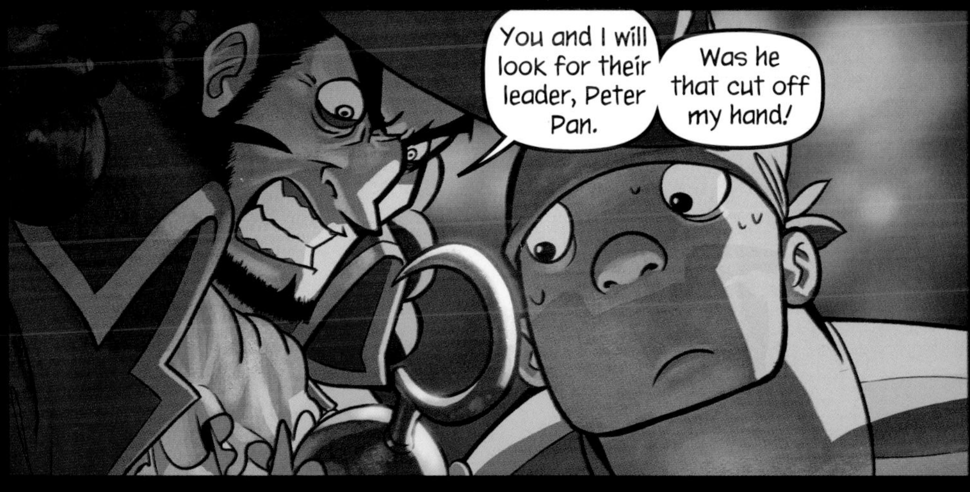
You and I will look for their leader, Peter Pan.
Was he that cut off my hand!

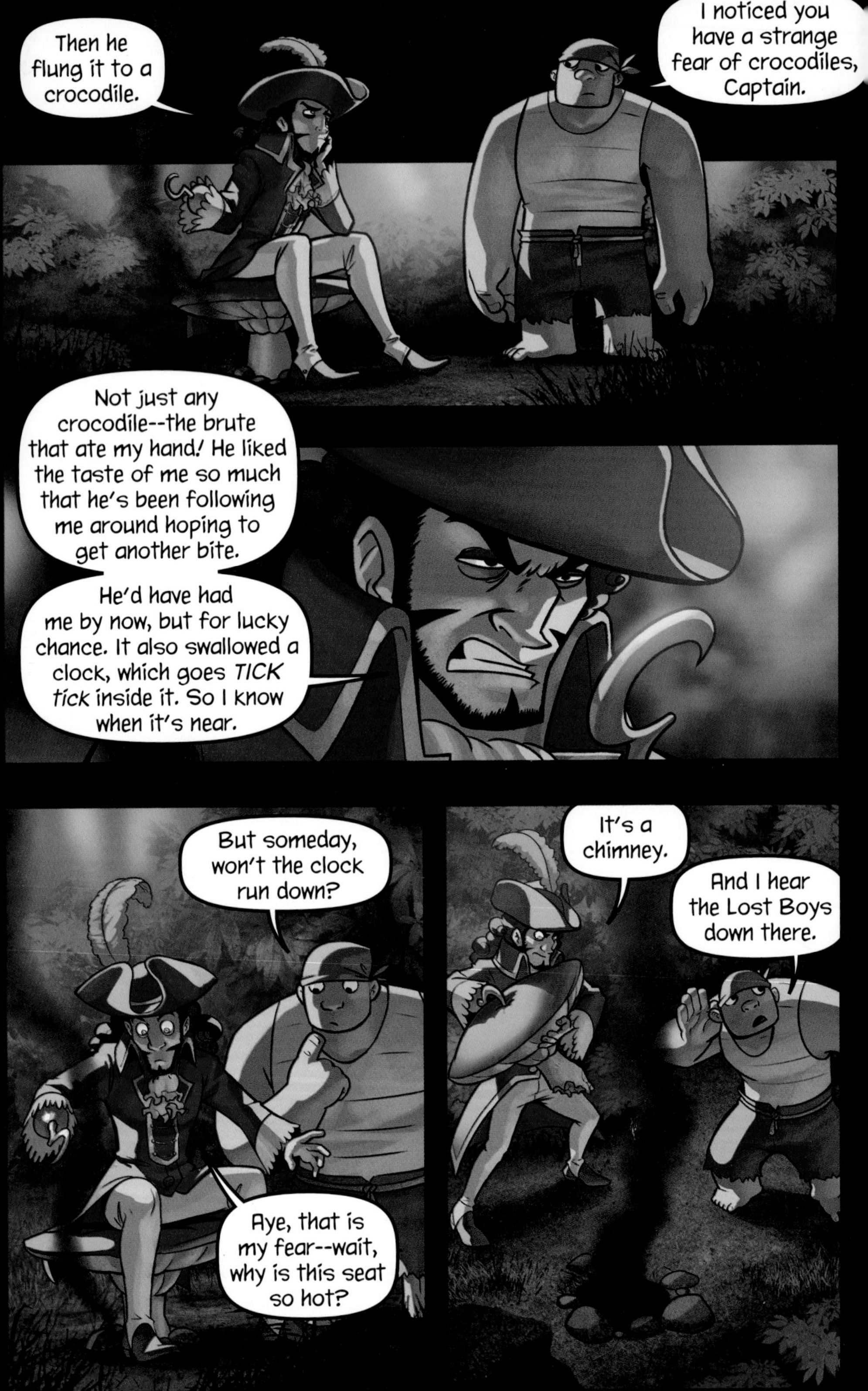
Then he flung it to a crocodile.
I noticed you have a strange fear of crocodiles, Captain.
Not just any crocodile--the brute that ate my hand! He liked the taste of me so much that he's been following me around hoping to get another bite.
He'd have had me by now, but for lucky chance. It also swallowed a clock, which goes *TICK tick* inside it. So I know when it's near.
But someday, won't the clock run down?
Aye, that is my fear--wait, why is this seat so hot?
It's a chimney.
And I hear the Lost Boys down there.

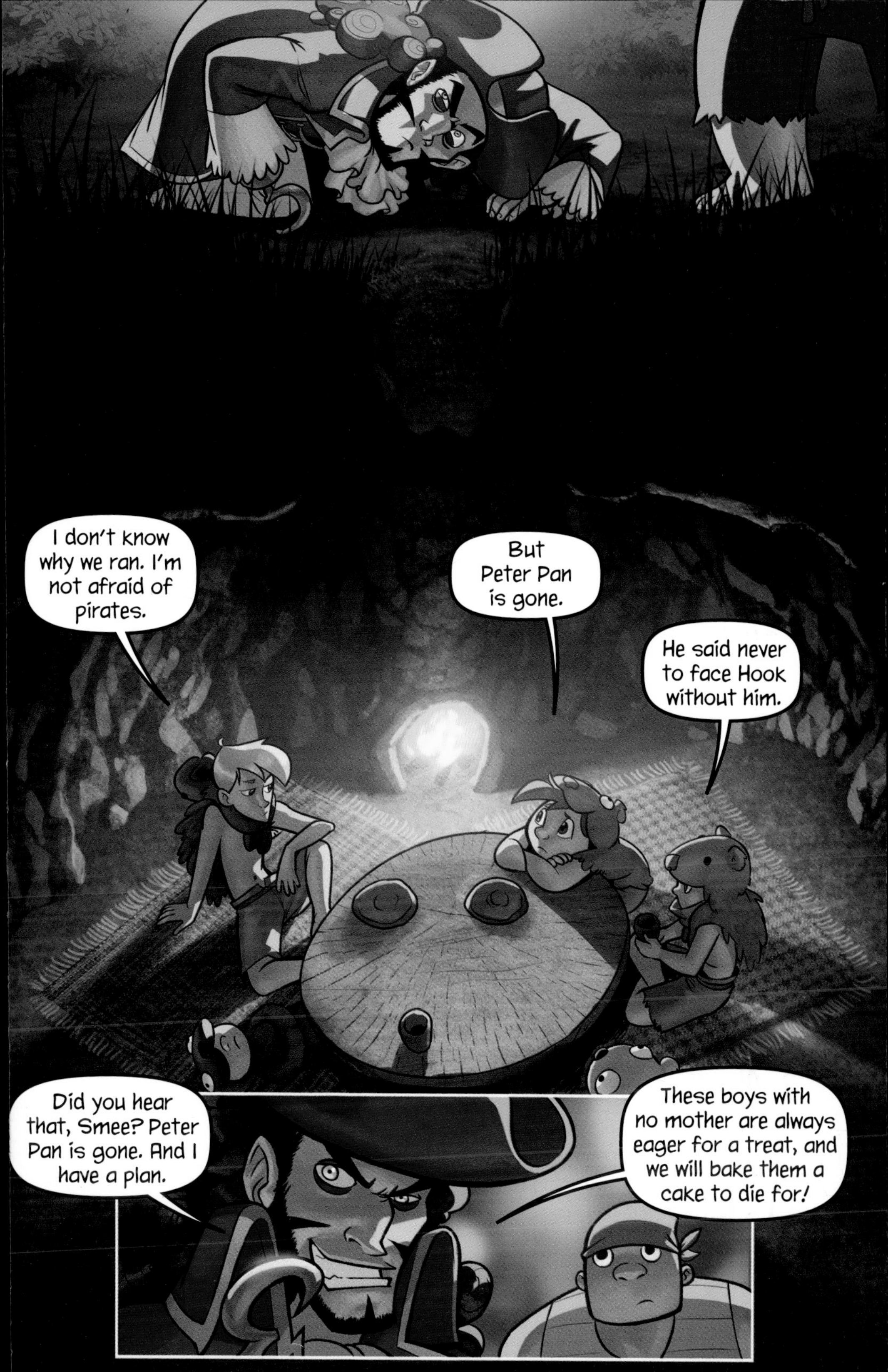
I don't know why we ran. I'm not afraid of pirates.
But Peter Pan is gone.
He said never to face Hook without him.
Did you hear that, Smee? Peter Pan is gone. And I have a plan.
These boys with no mother are always eager for a treat, and we will bake them a cake to die for!

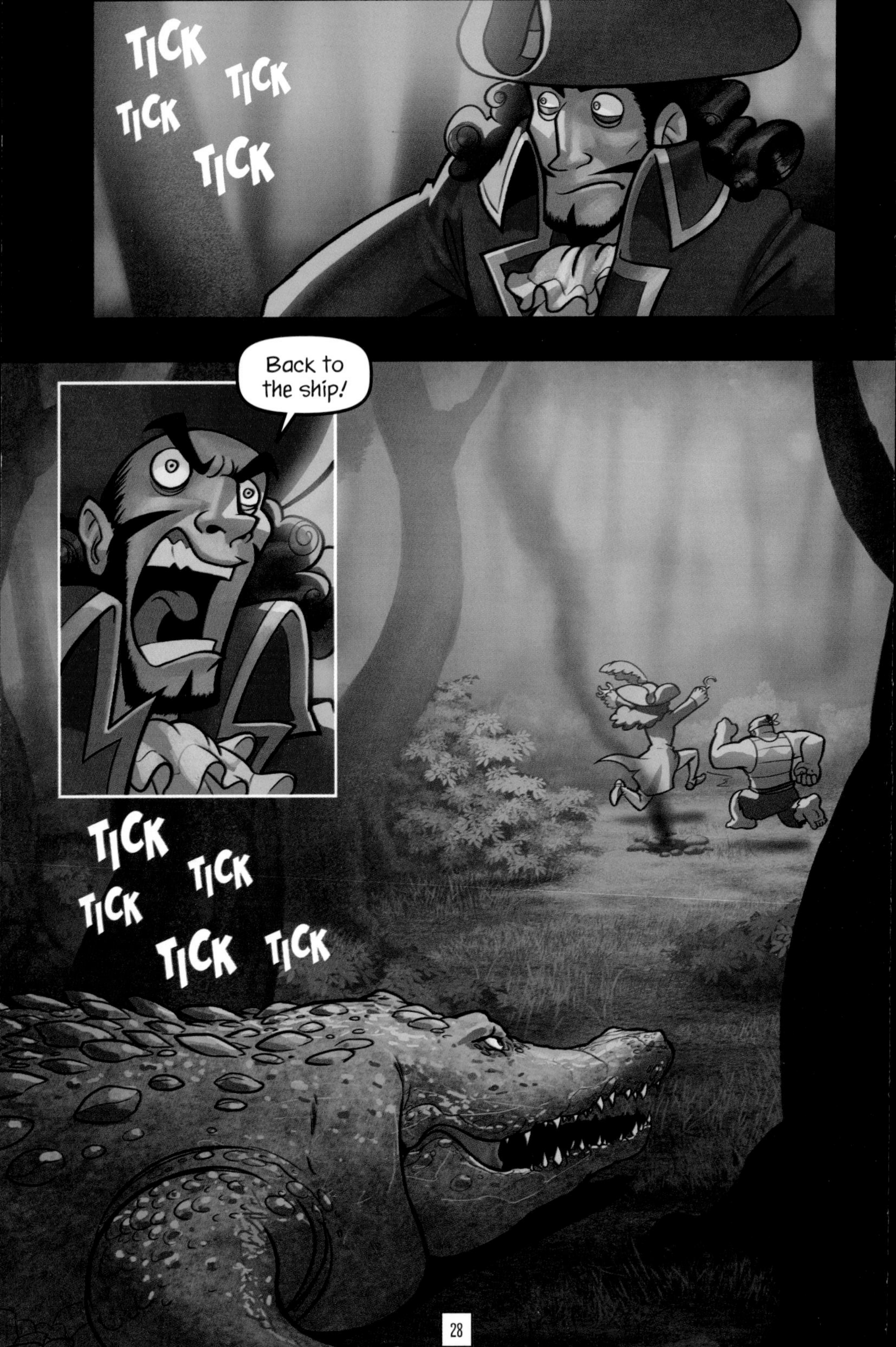
TICK
TICK
TICK
TICK
Back to the ship!
TICK
TICK
TICK
TICK
TICK

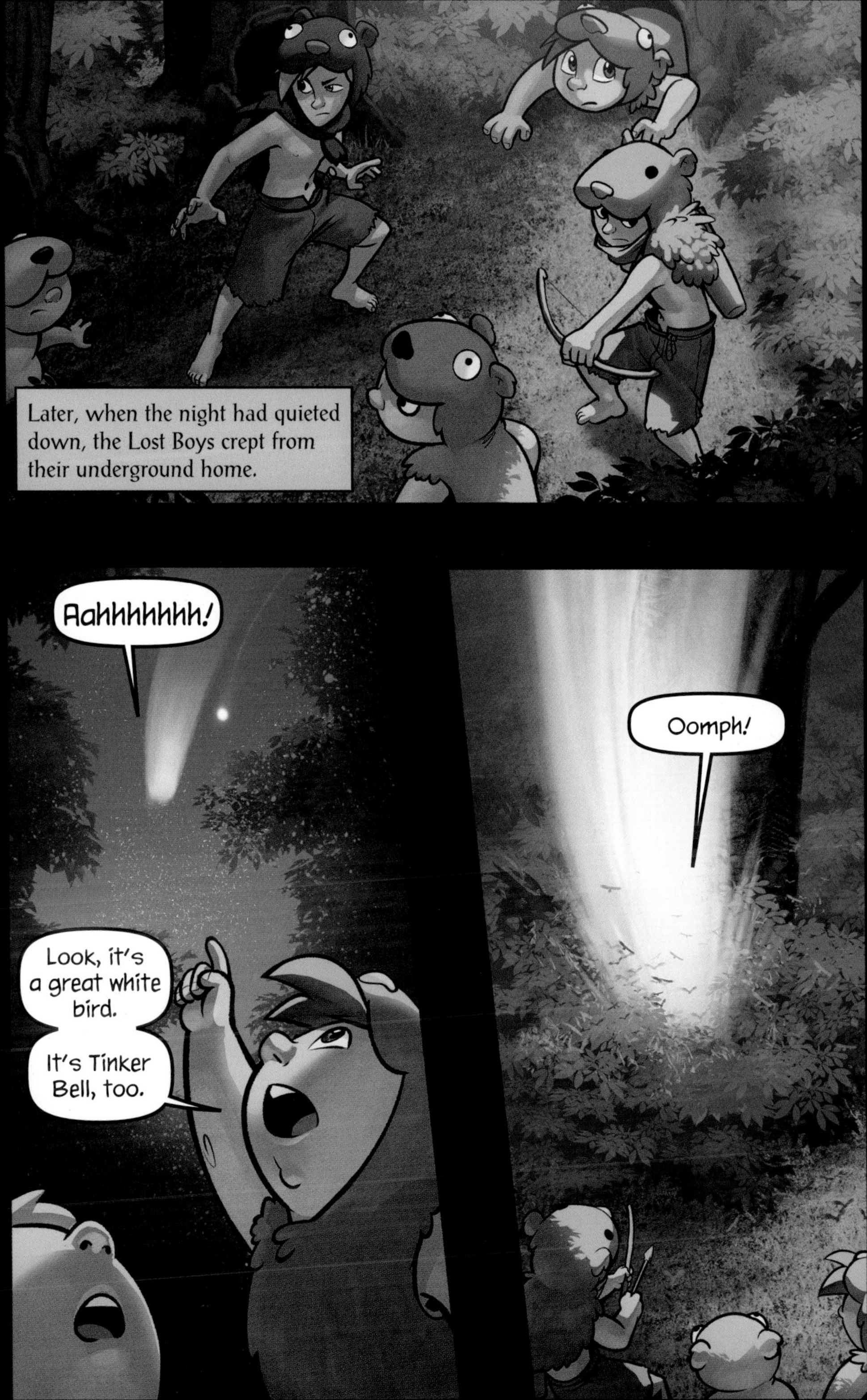
Later, when the night had quieted down, the Lost Boys crept from their underground home.
Aahhhhhh!
Look, it's a great white bird.
It's Tinker Bell, too.
Oomph!

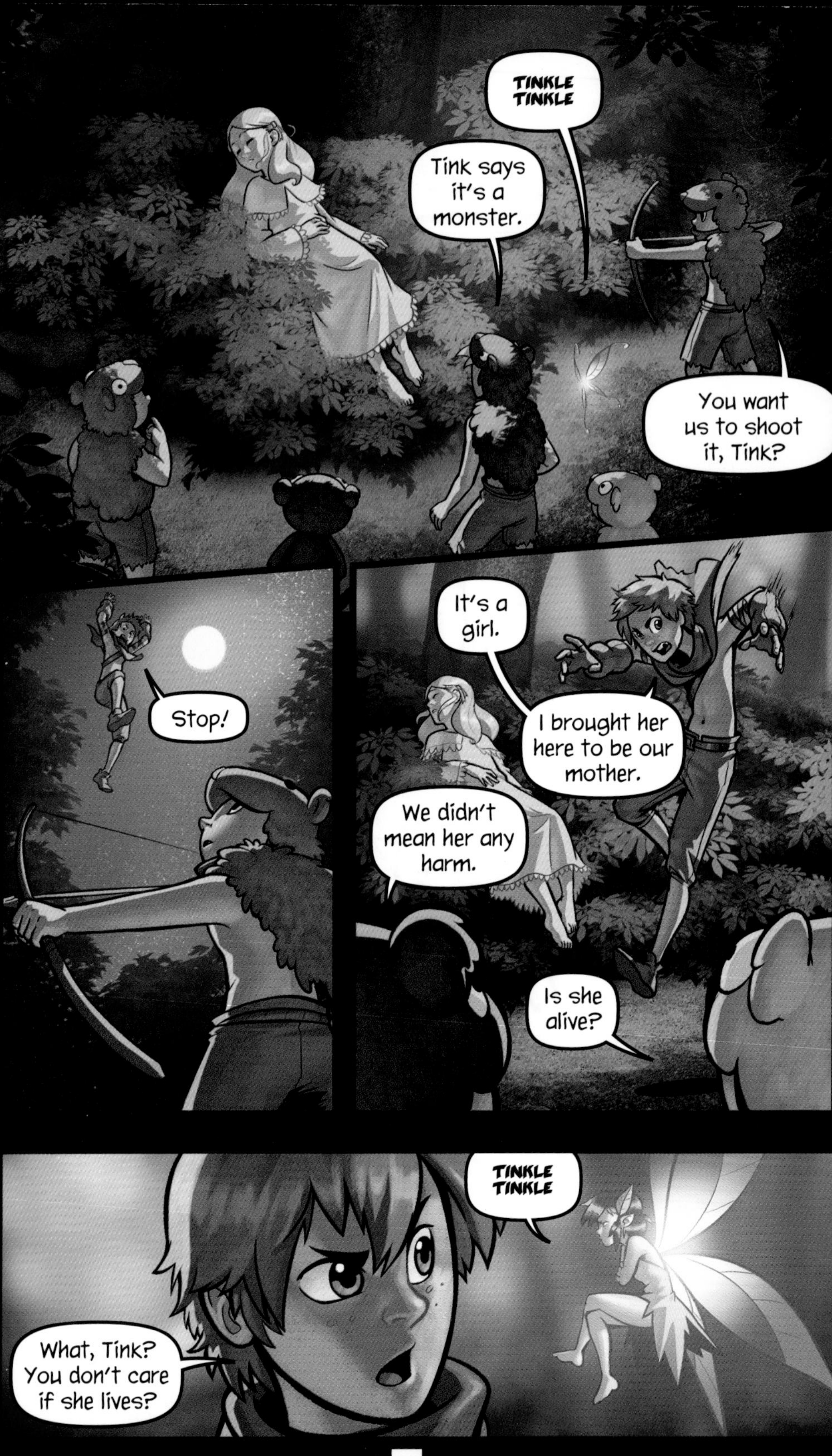
TINKLE TINKLE
Tink says it's a monster.
You want us to shoot it, Tink?
Stop!
It's a girl.
I brought her here to be our mother.
We didn't mean her any harm.
Is she alive?
TINKLE TINKLE
What, Tink? You don't care if she lives?

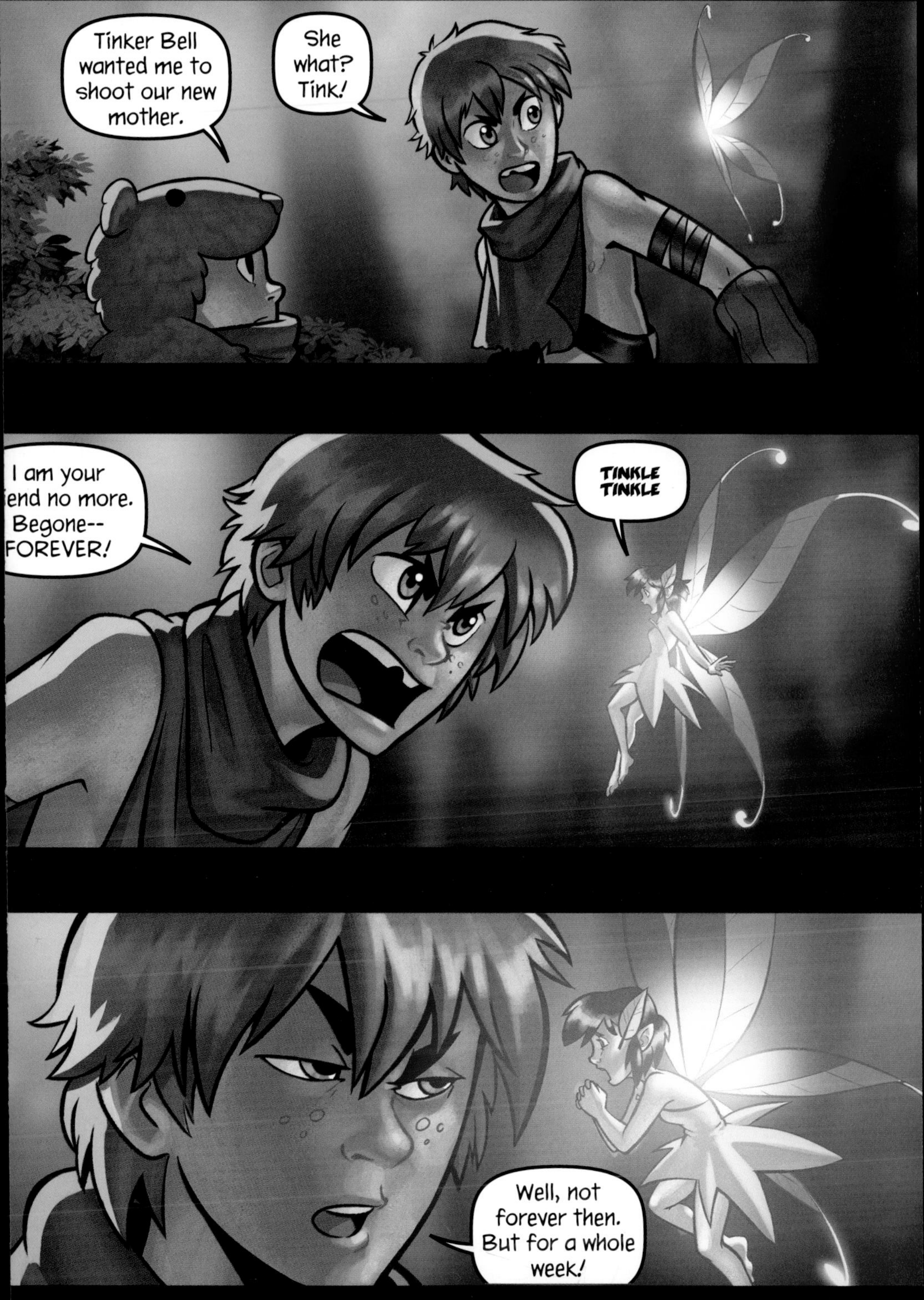
Tinker Bell wanted me to shoot our new mother.
She what? Tink!
I am your iend no more. Begone-- FOREVER!
TINKLE TINKLE
Well, not forever then. But for a whole week!

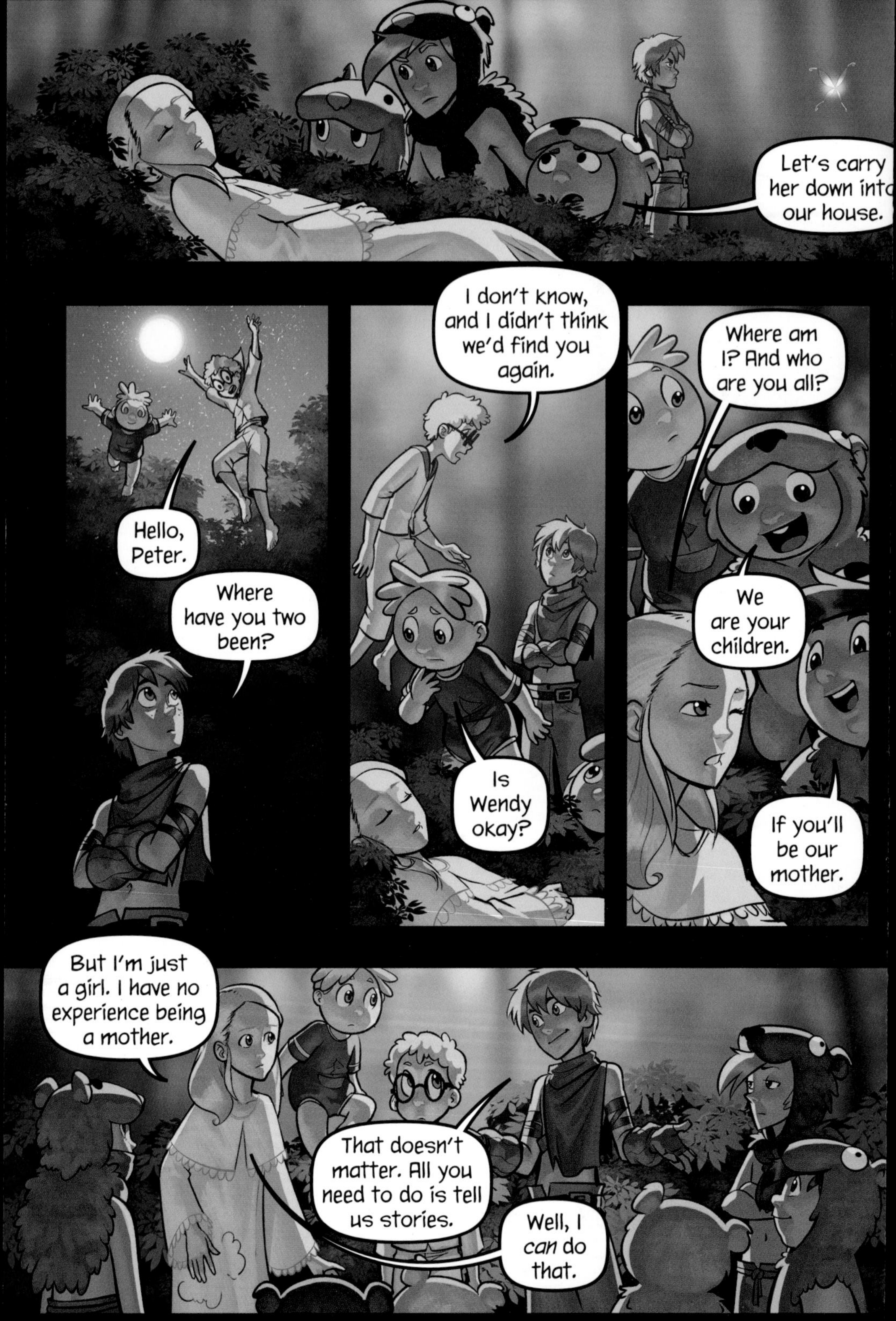
Let's carry her down into our house.
Hello, Peter.
Where have you two been?
I don't know, and I didn't think we'd find you again.
Is Wendy okay?
Where am I? And who are you all?
We are your children.
If you'll be our mother.
But I'm just a girl. I have no experience being a mother.
That doesn't matter. All you need to do is tell us stories.
Well, I *can* do that.

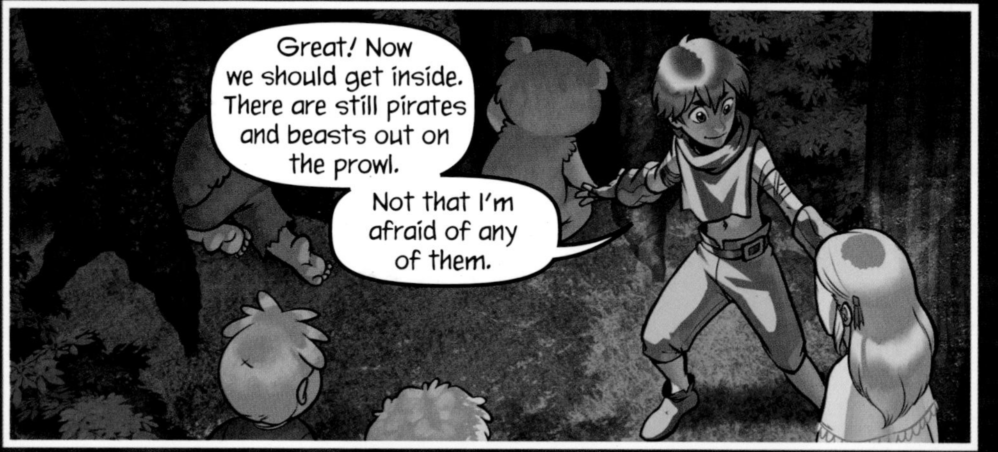
Great! Now we should get inside. There are still pirates and beasts out on the prowl.
Not that I'm afraid of any of them.

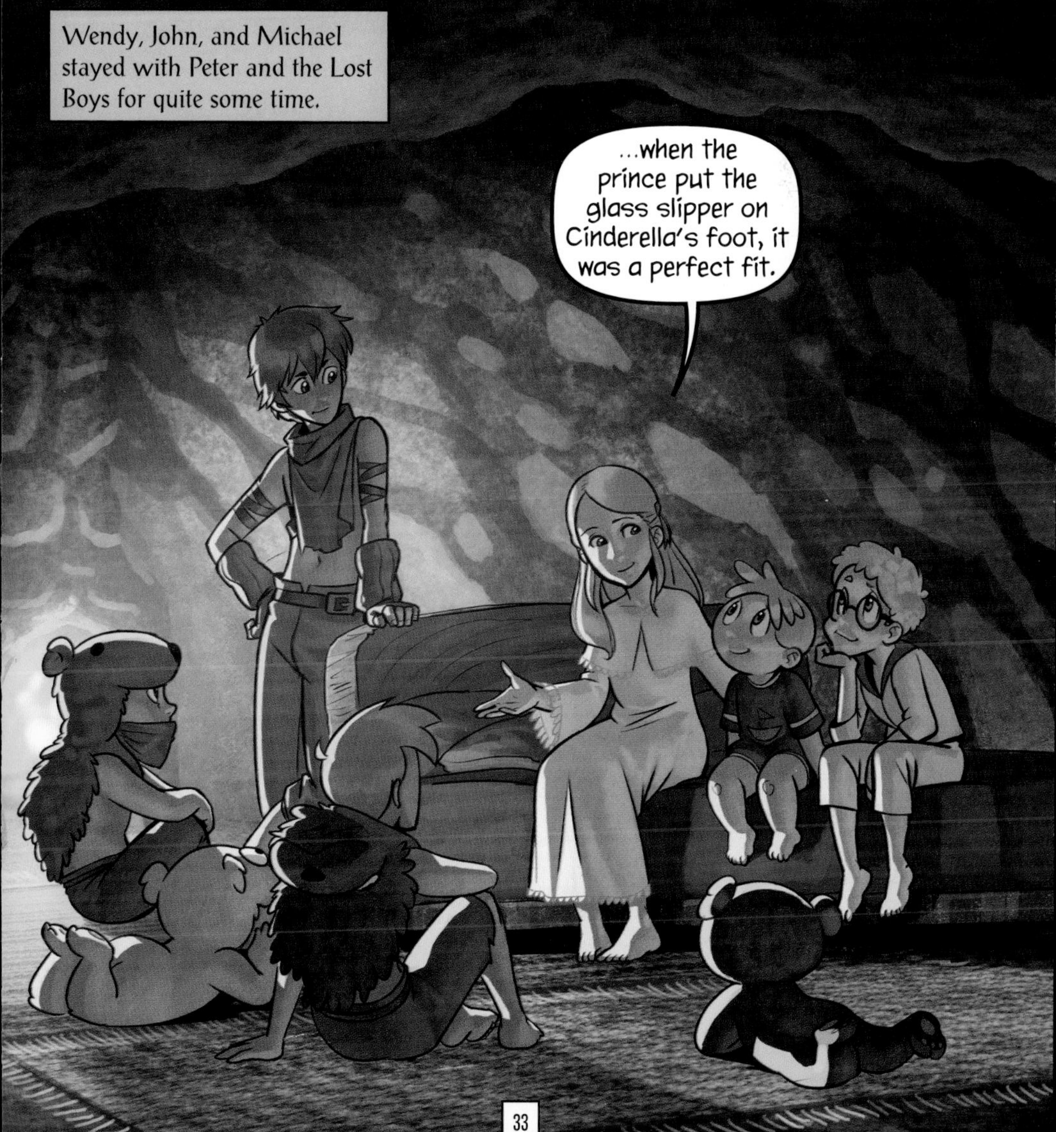
Wendy, John, and Michael stayed with Peter and the Lost Boys for quite some time.
...when the prince put the glass slipper on Cinderella's foot, it was a perfect fit.

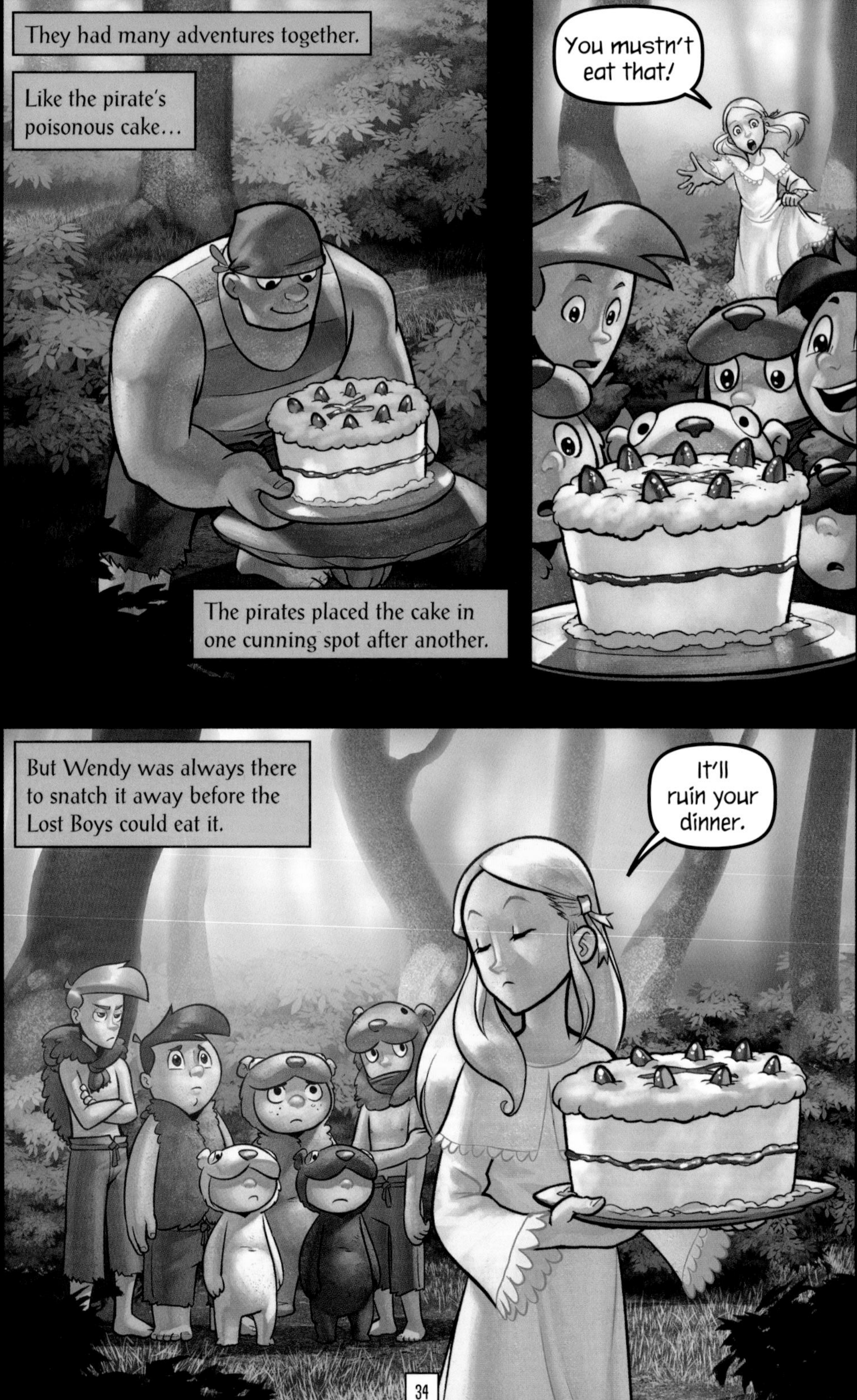
They had many adventures together.
Like the pirate's poisonous cake...
The pirates placed the cake in one cunning spot after another.
You mustn't eat that!
But Wendy was always there to snatch it away before the Lost Boys could eat it.
It'll ruin your dinner.

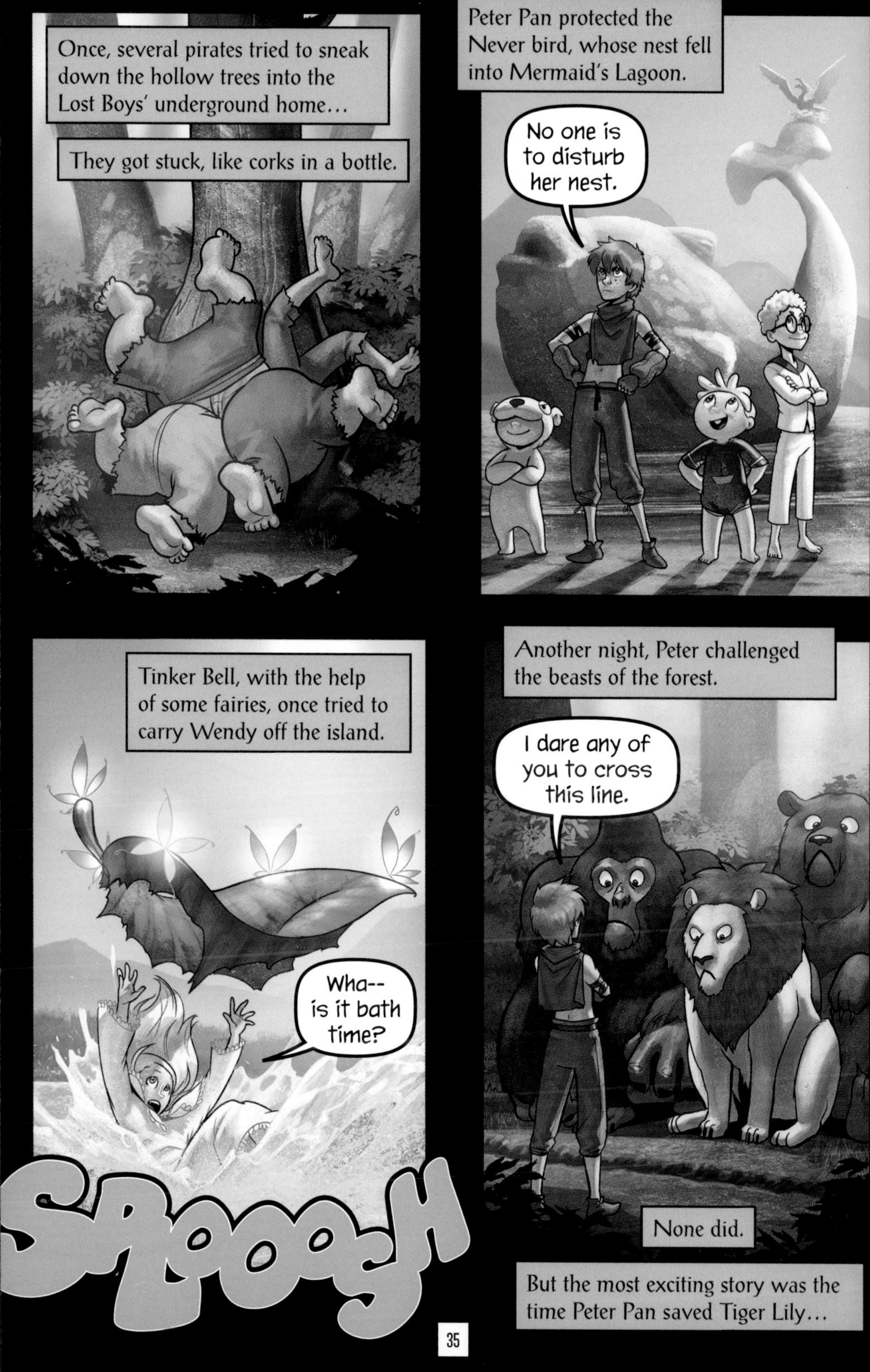

Once, several pirates tried to sneak down the hollow trees into the Lost Boys' underground home...
They got stuck, like corks in a bottle.
Peter Pan protected the Never bird, whose nest fell into Mermaid's Lagoon.
No one is to disturb her nest.
Tinker Bell, with the help of some fairies, once tried to carry Wendy off the island.
Wha-- is it bath time?
SPLOOOSH
Another night, Peter challenged the beasts of the forest.
I dare any of you to cross this line.
None did.
But the most exciting story was the time Peter Pan saved Tiger Lily...

CHAPTER 3
TIGER LILY

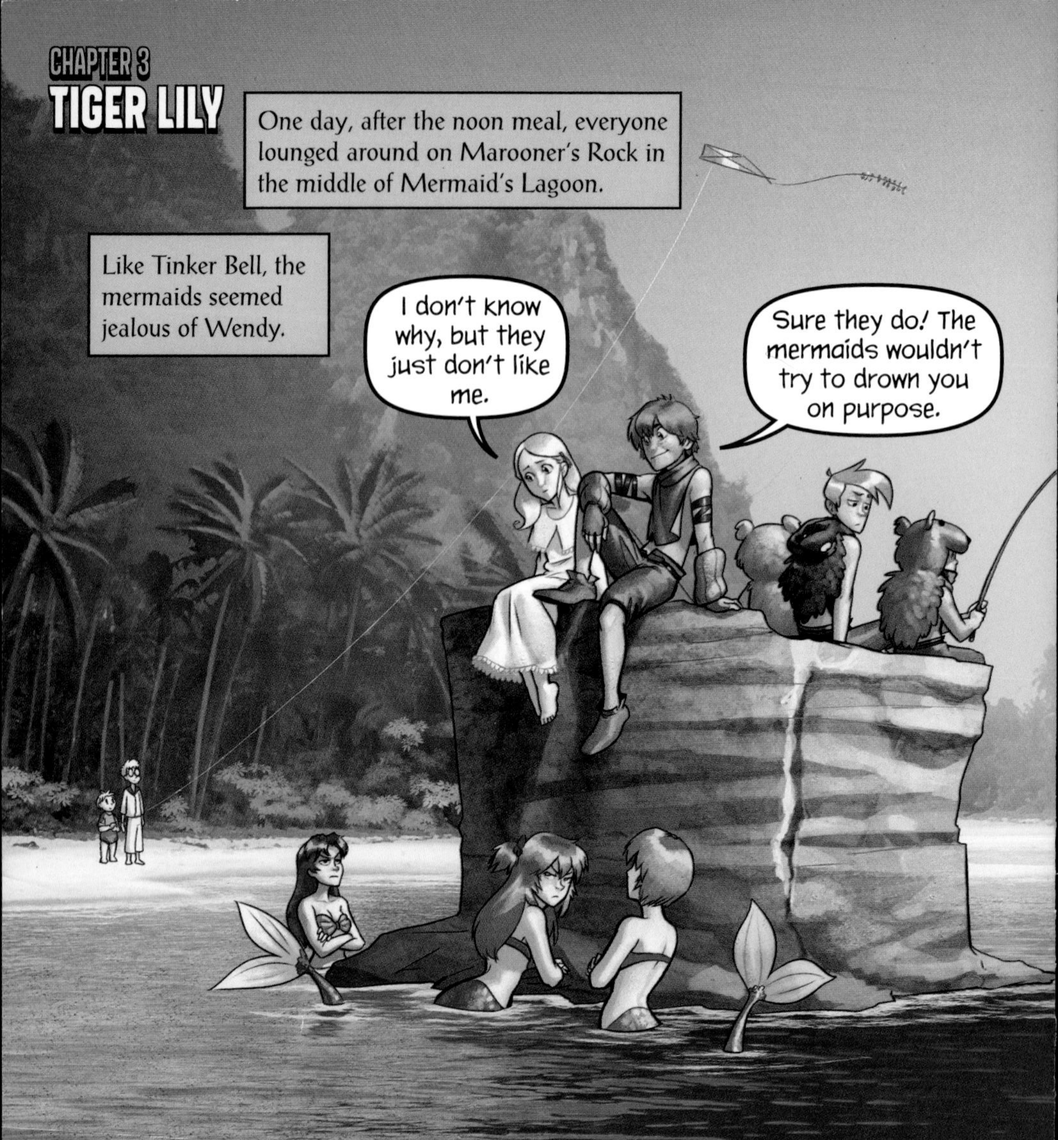
One day, after the noon meal, everyone lounged around on Marooner's Rock in the middle of Mermaid's Lagoon.
Like Tinker Bell, the mermaids seemed jealous of Wendy.
I don't know why, but they just don't like me.
Sure they do! The mermaids wouldn't try to drown you on purpose.

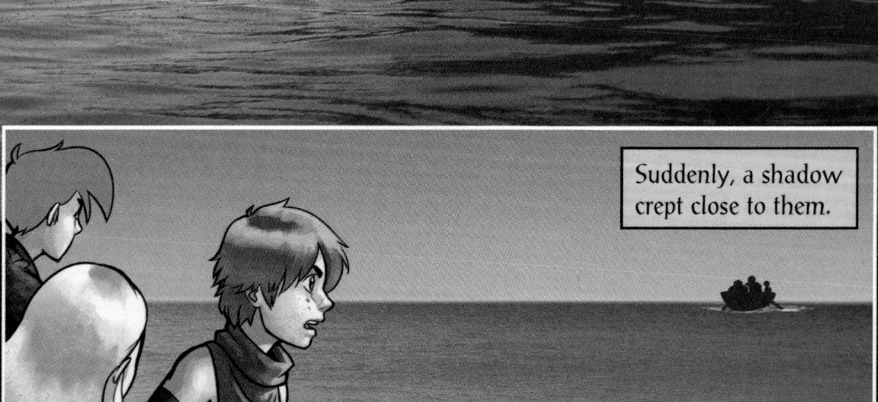
Suddenly, a shadow crept close to them.

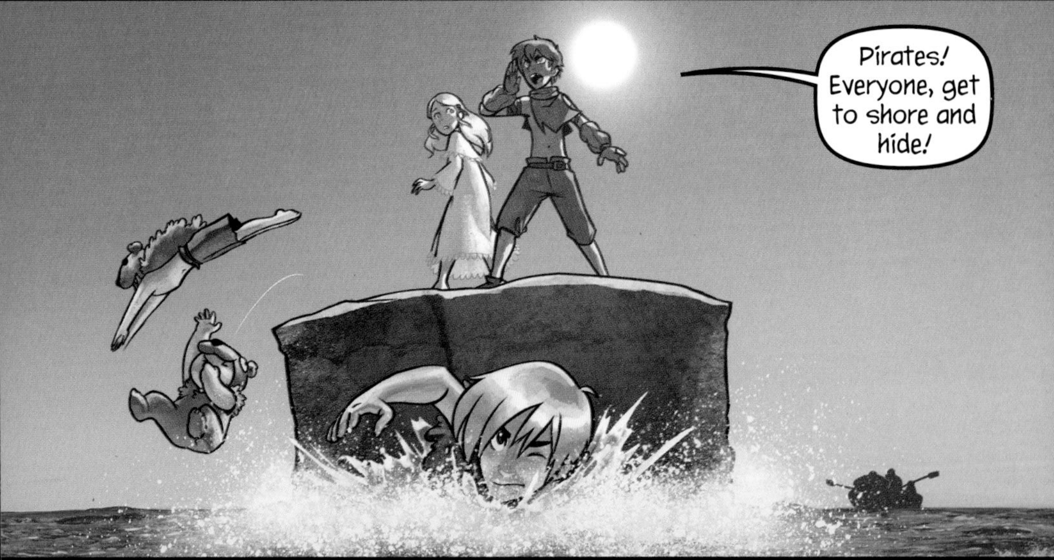
Pirates! Everyone, get to shore and hide!

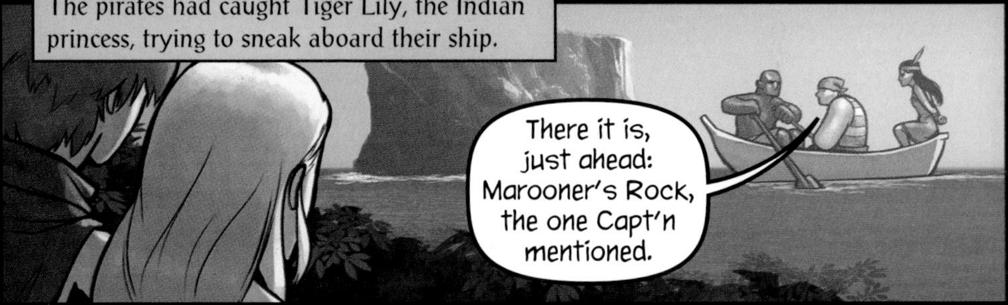
The pirates had caught Tiger Lily, the Indian princess, trying to sneak aboard their ship.
There it is, just ahead: Marooner's Rock, the one Capt'n mentioned.

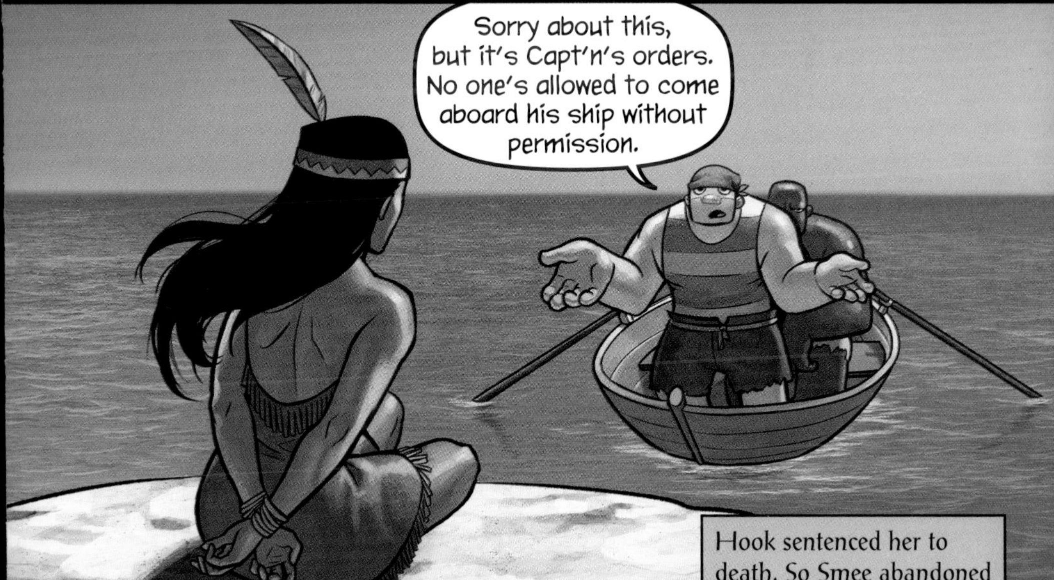
Sorry about this, but it's Capt'n's orders. No one's allowed to come aboard his ship without permission.
Hook sentenced her to death. So Smee abandoned her on Marooner's Rock.

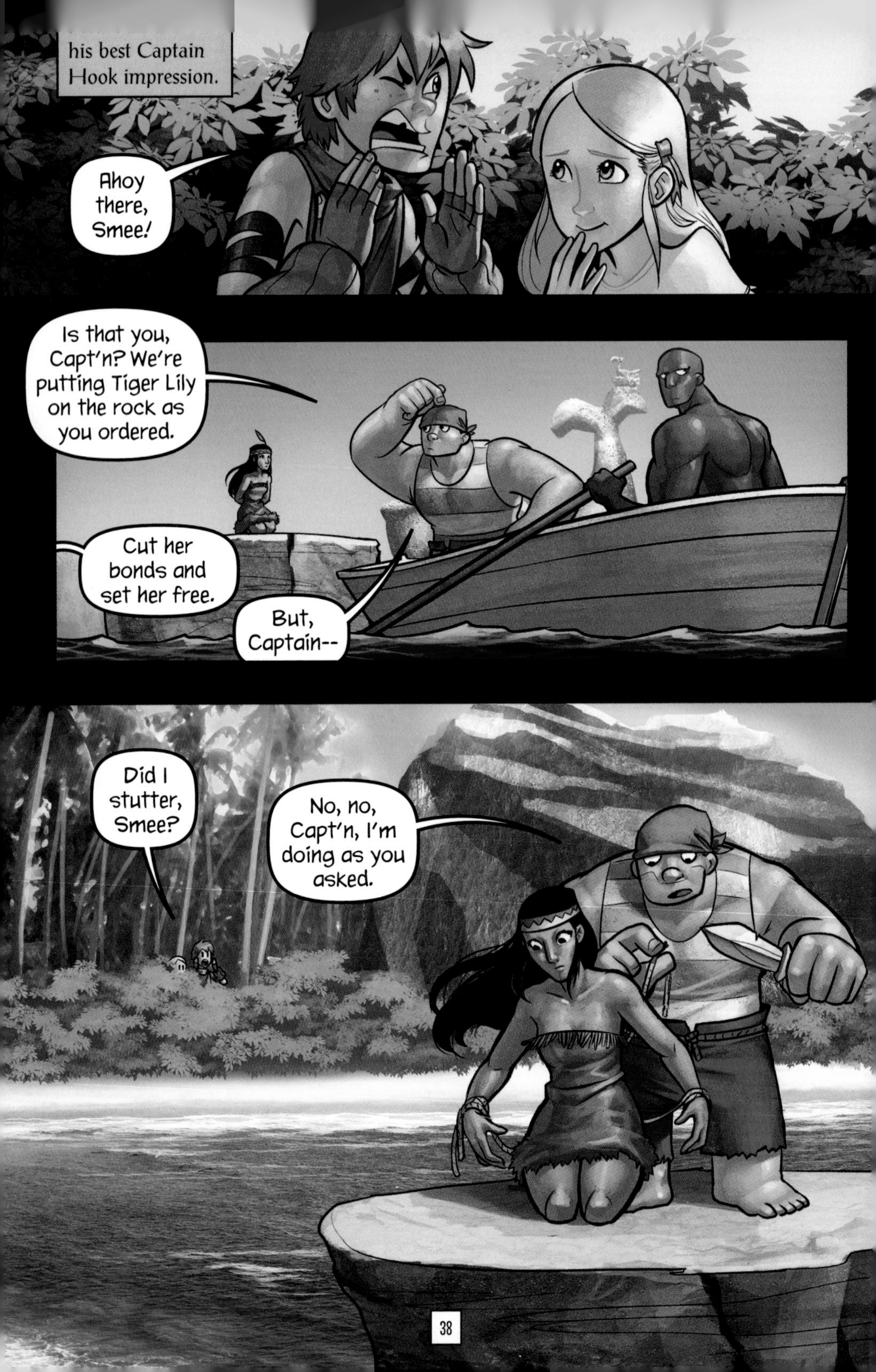
his best Captain Hook impression.
Ahoy there, Smee!
Is that you, Capt'n? We're putting Tiger Lily on the rock as you ordered.
Cut her bonds and set her free.
But, Captain--
Did I stutter, Smee?
No, no, Capt'n, I'm doing as you asked.

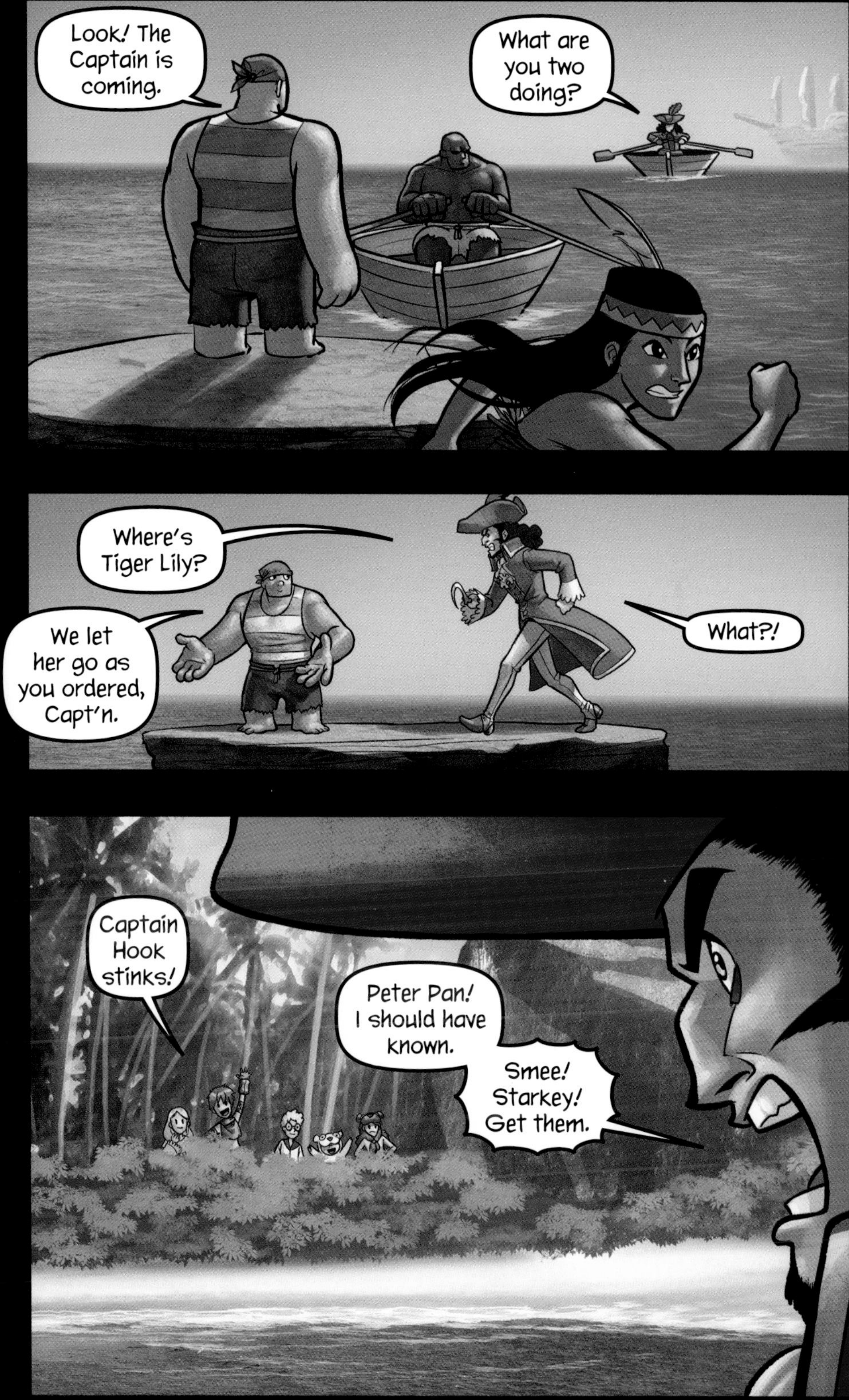
Look! The Captain is coming.
What are you two doing?
Where's Tiger Lily?
We let her go as you ordered, Capt'n.
What?!
Captain Hook stinks!
Peter Pan! I should have known.
Smee! Starkey! Get them.

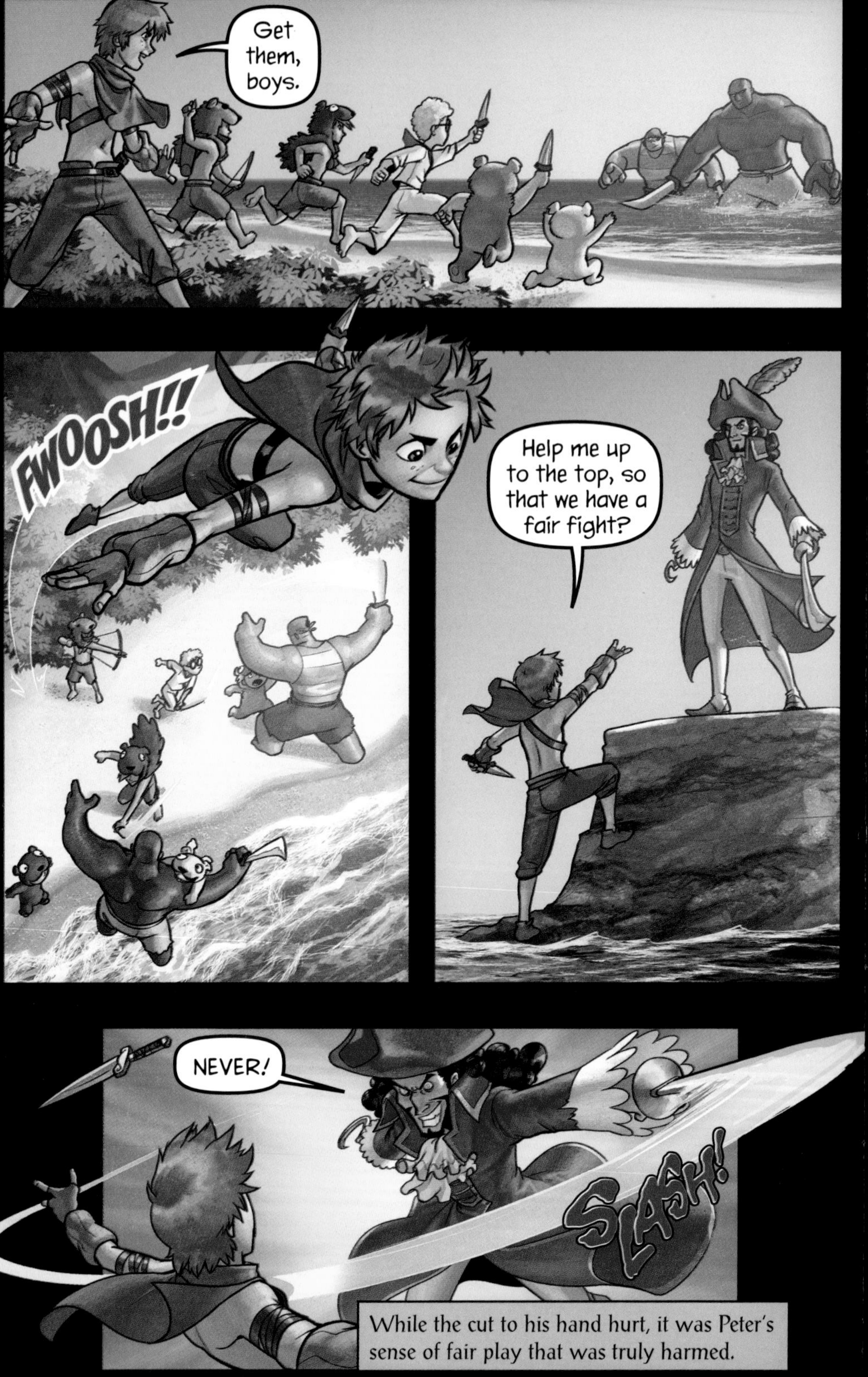
Get them, boys.
FWOOSH!!
Help me up to the top, so that we have a fair fight?
NEVER!
SLASH!
While the cut to his hand hurt, it was Peter's sense of fair play that was truly harmed.

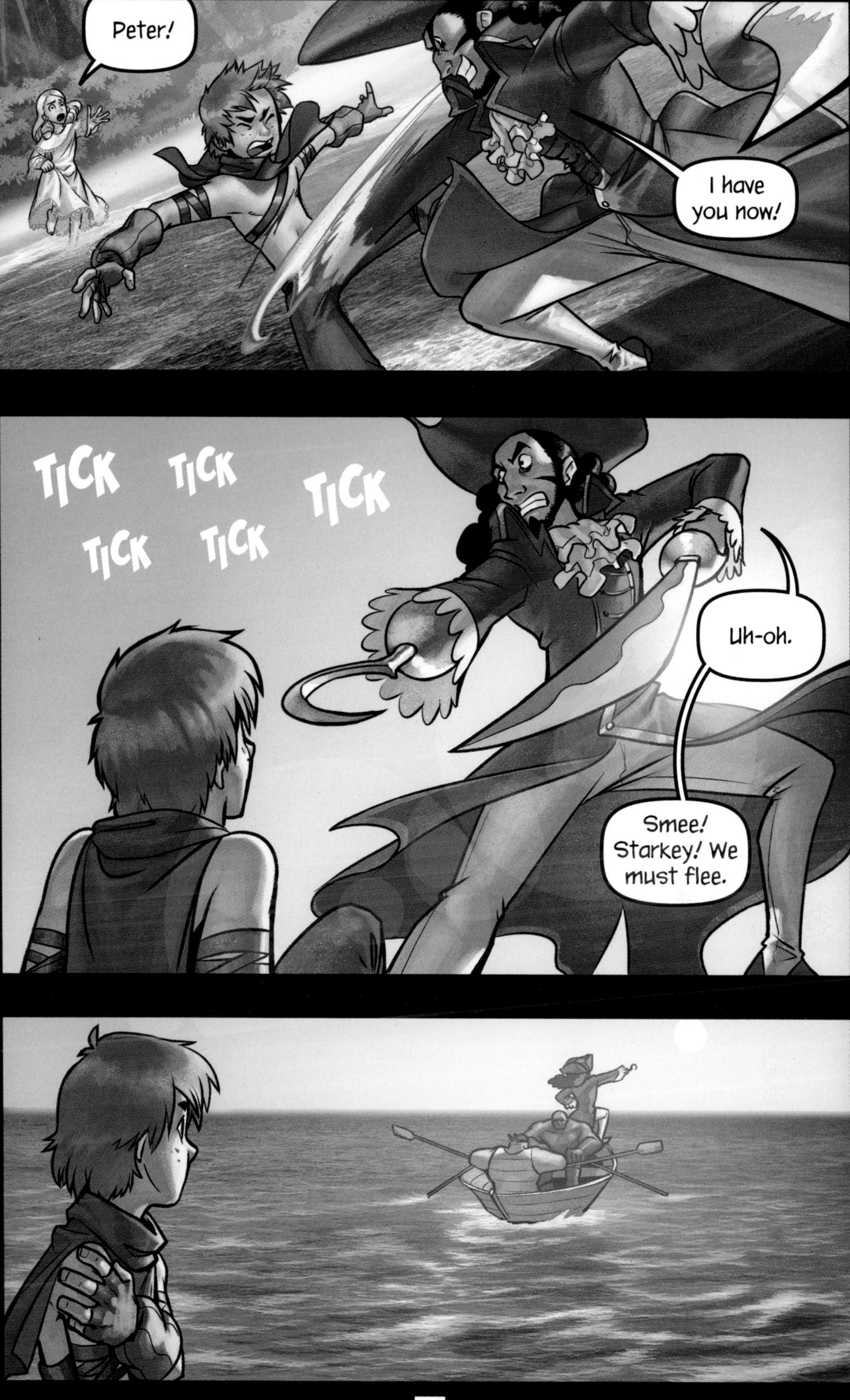

Peter!
I have you now!
TICK
TICK
TICK
TICK
TICK
Uh-oh.
Smee! Starkey! We must flee.

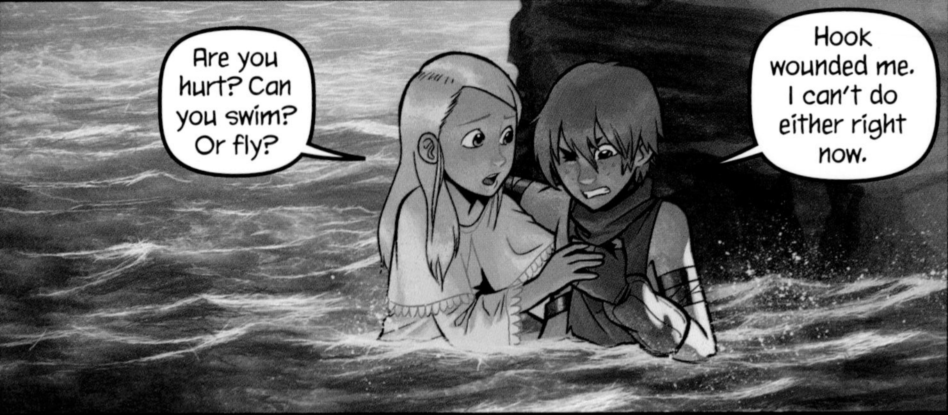
Are you hurt? Can you swim? Or fly?
Hook wounded me. I can't do either right now.

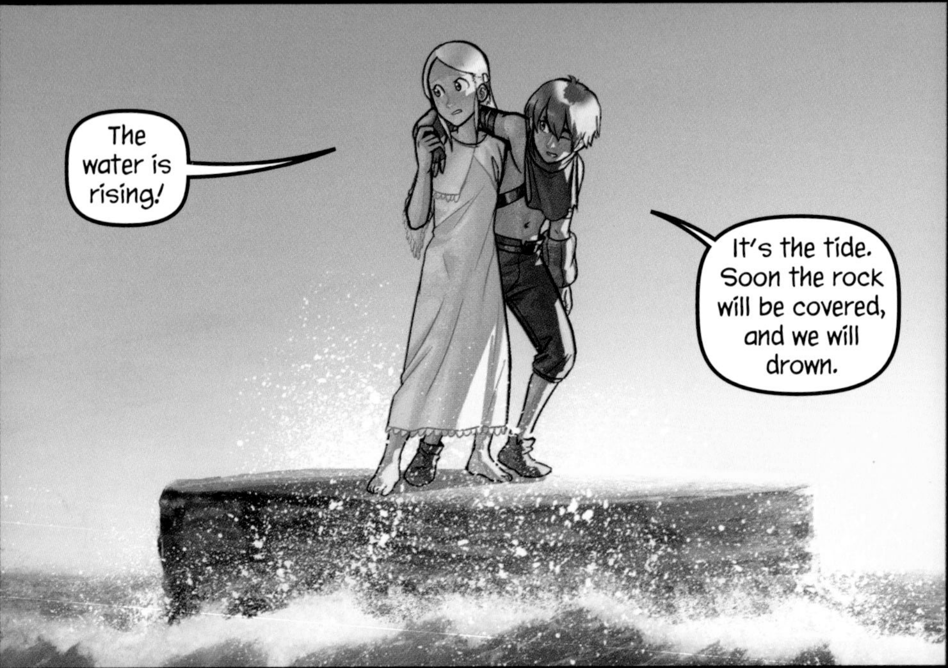
The water is rising!
It's the tide. Soon the rock will be covered, and we will drown.

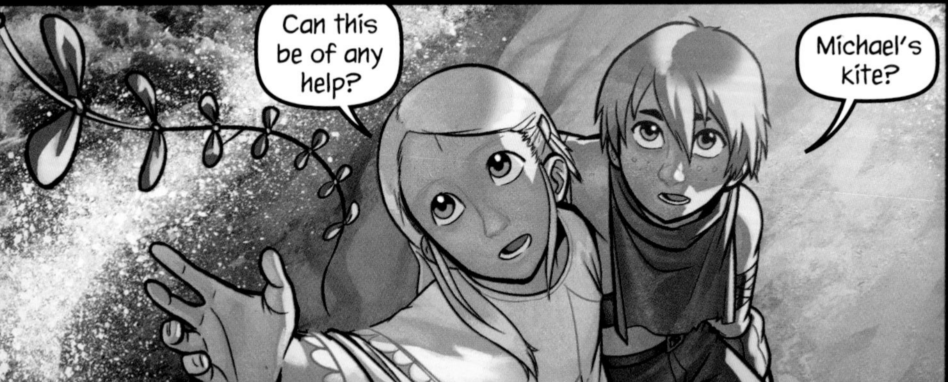
Can this be of any help?
Michael's kite?

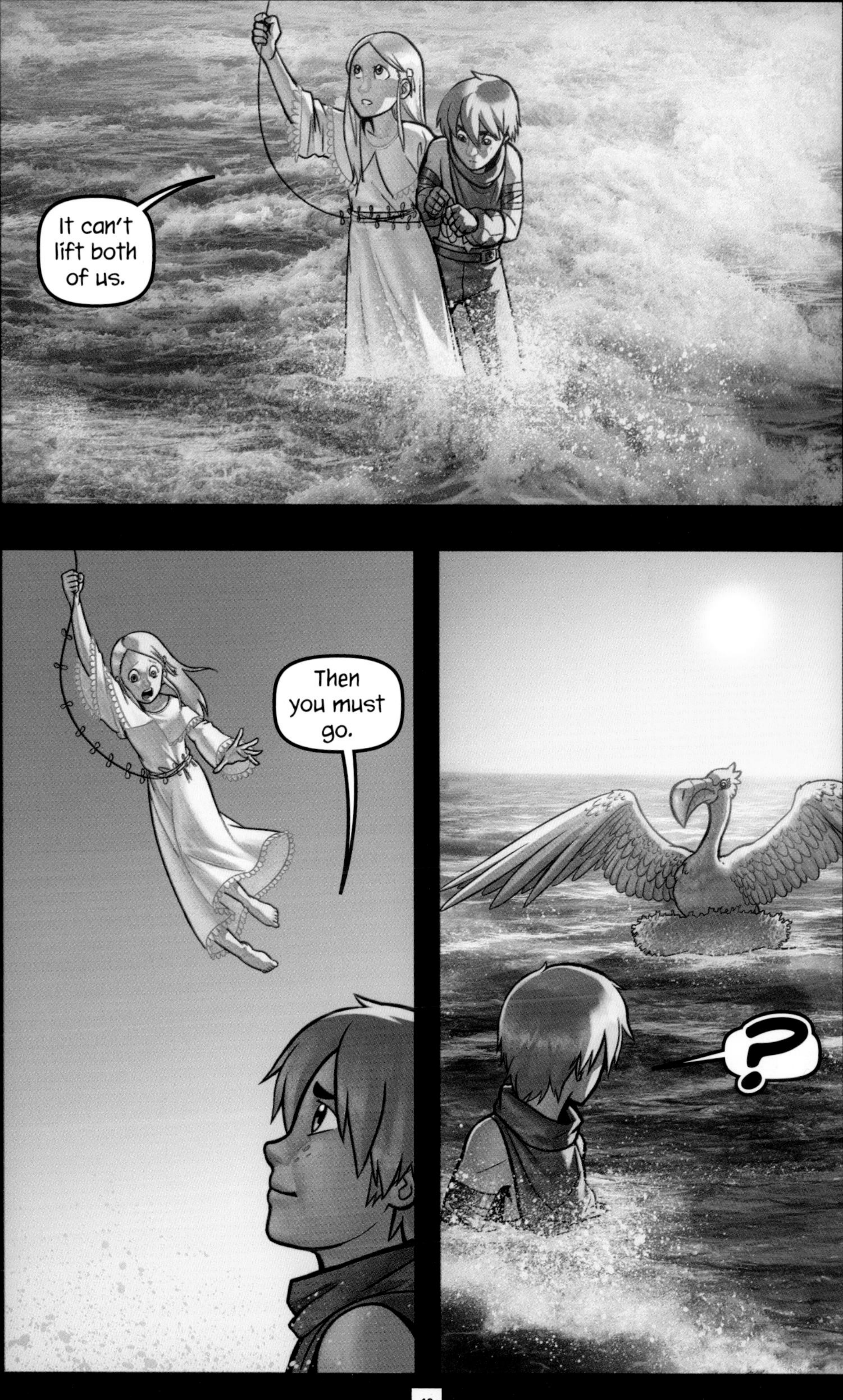
It can't lift both of us.
Then you must go.
?

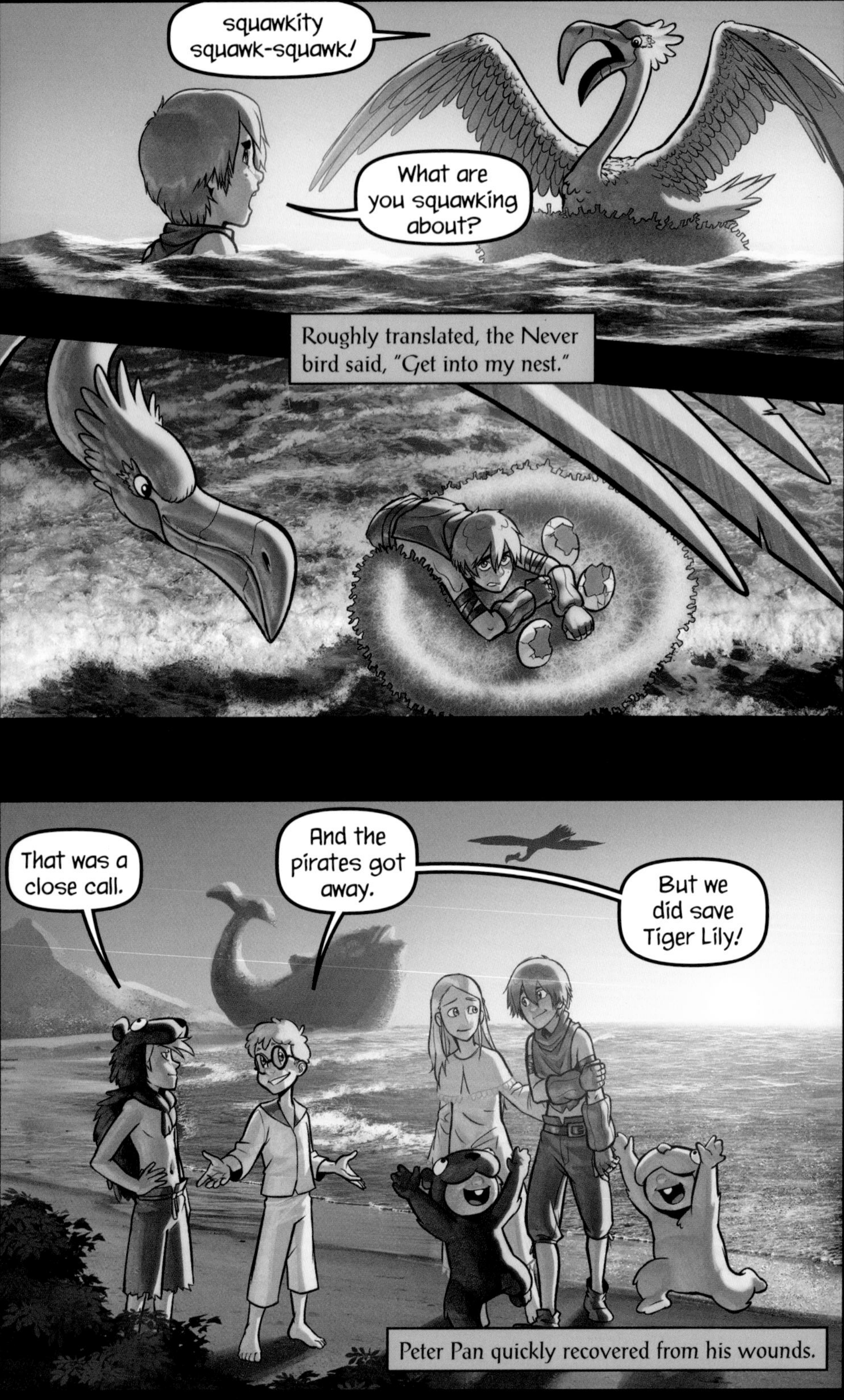
squawkity squawk-squawk!
What are you squawking about?
Roughly translated, the Never bird said, "Get into my nest."
That was a close call.
And the pirates got away.
But we did save Tiger Lily!
Peter Pan quickly recovered from his wounds.

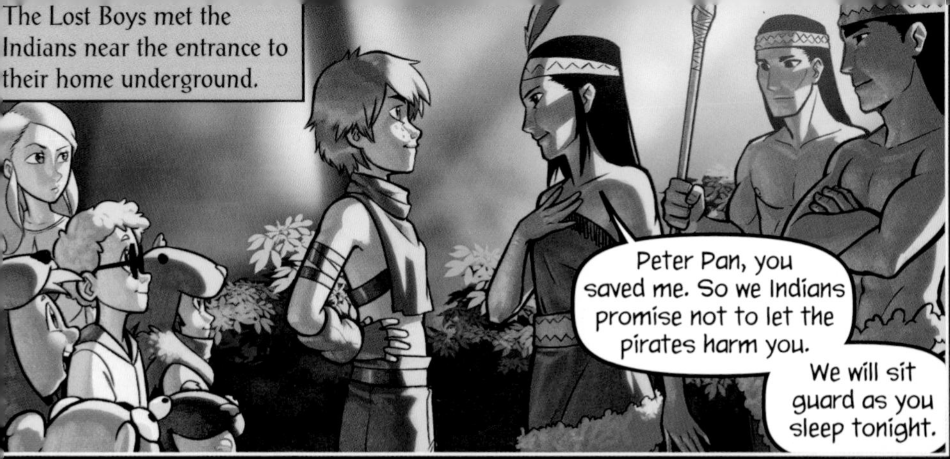
The Lost Boys met the Indians near the entrance to their home underground.
Peter Pan, you saved me. So we Indians promise not to let the pirates harm you.
We will sit guard as you sleep tonight.

CHAPTER 4

WENDY'S STORY

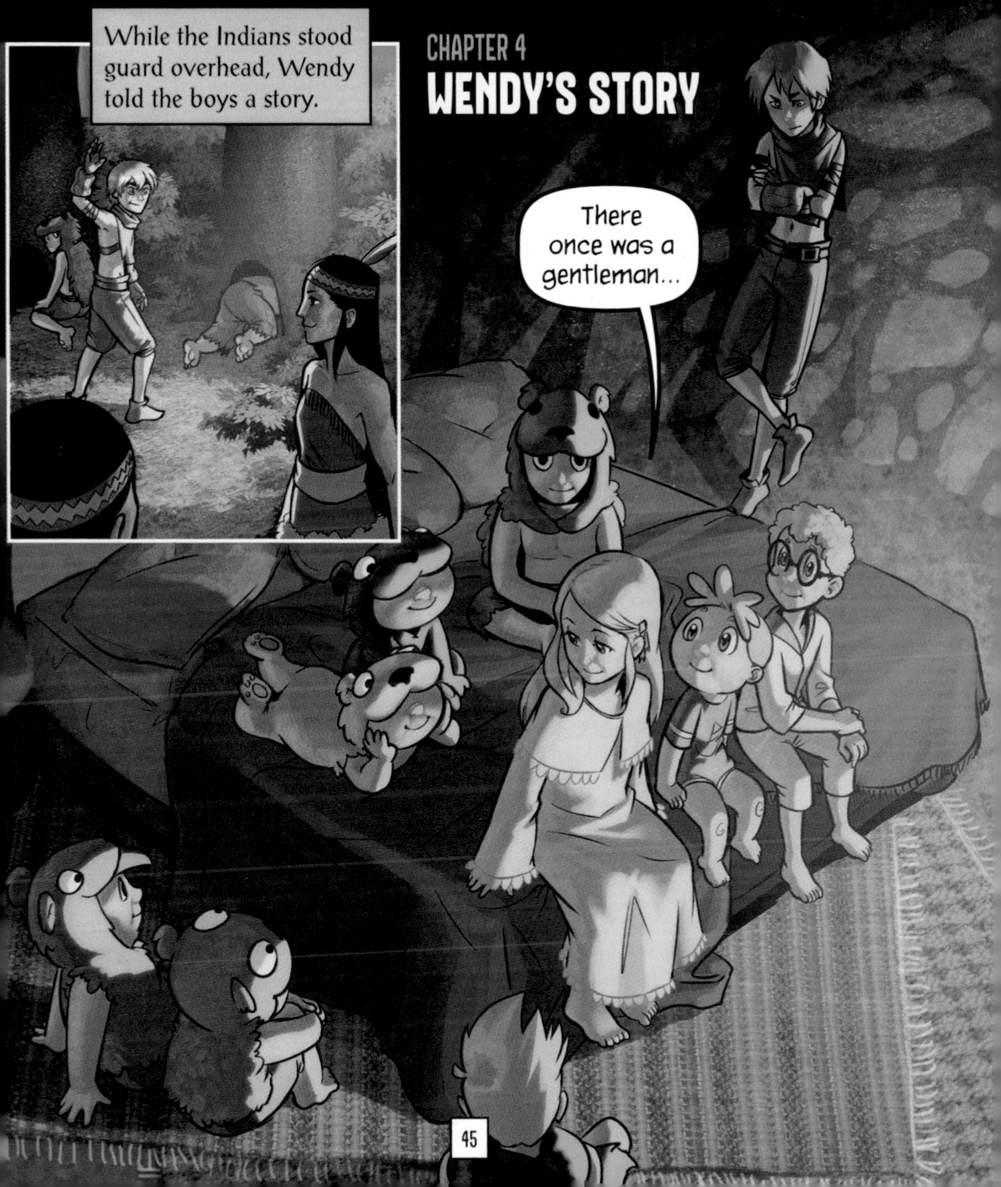
While the Indians stood guard overhead, Wendy told the boys a story.
There once was a gentleman...

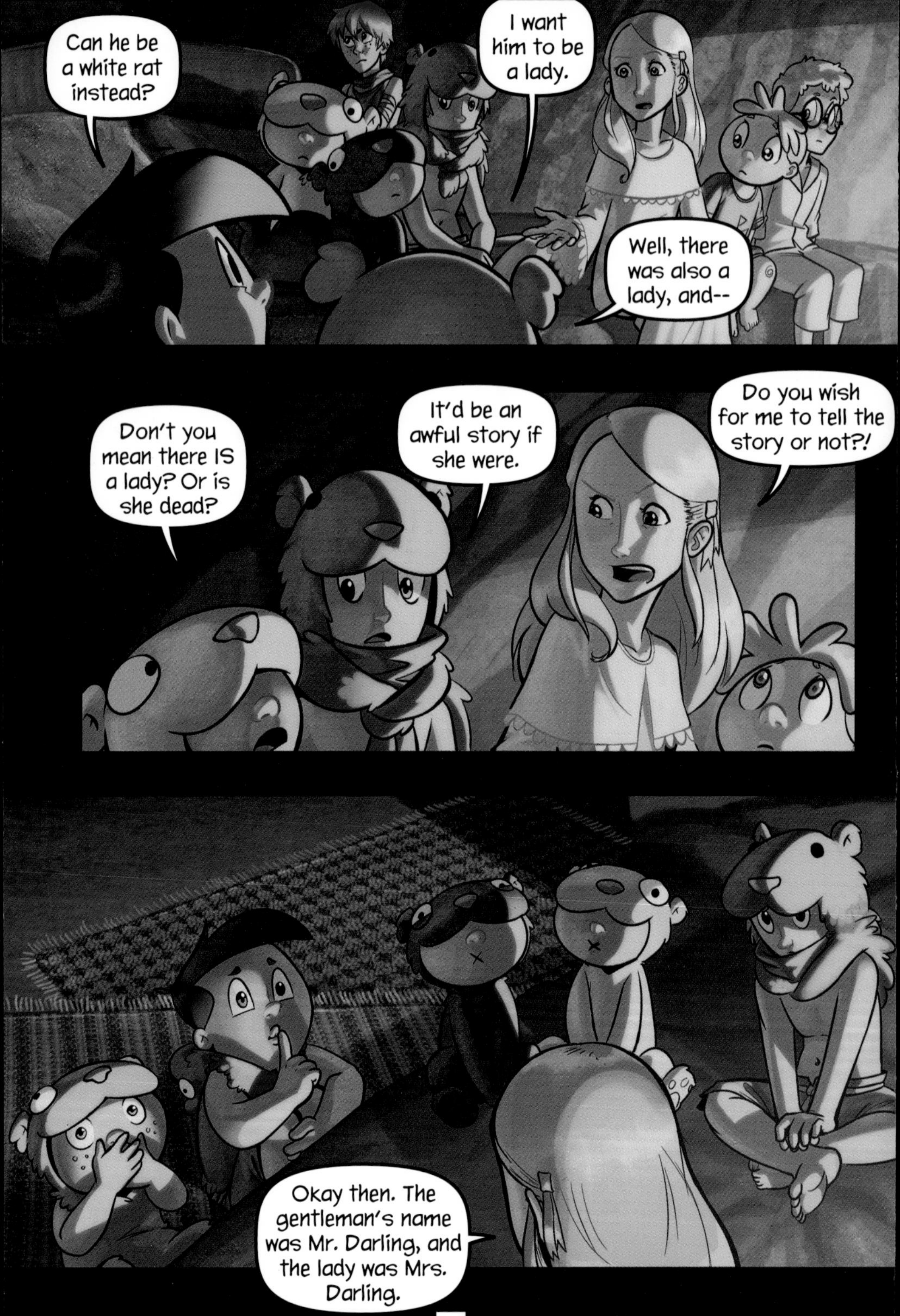
Can he be a white rat instead?
I want him to be a lady.
Well, there was also a lady, and--
Don't you mean there IS a lady? Or is she dead?
It'd be an awful story if she were.
Do you wish for me to tell the story or not?!
Okay then. The gentleman's name was Mr. Darling, and the lady was Mrs. Darling.

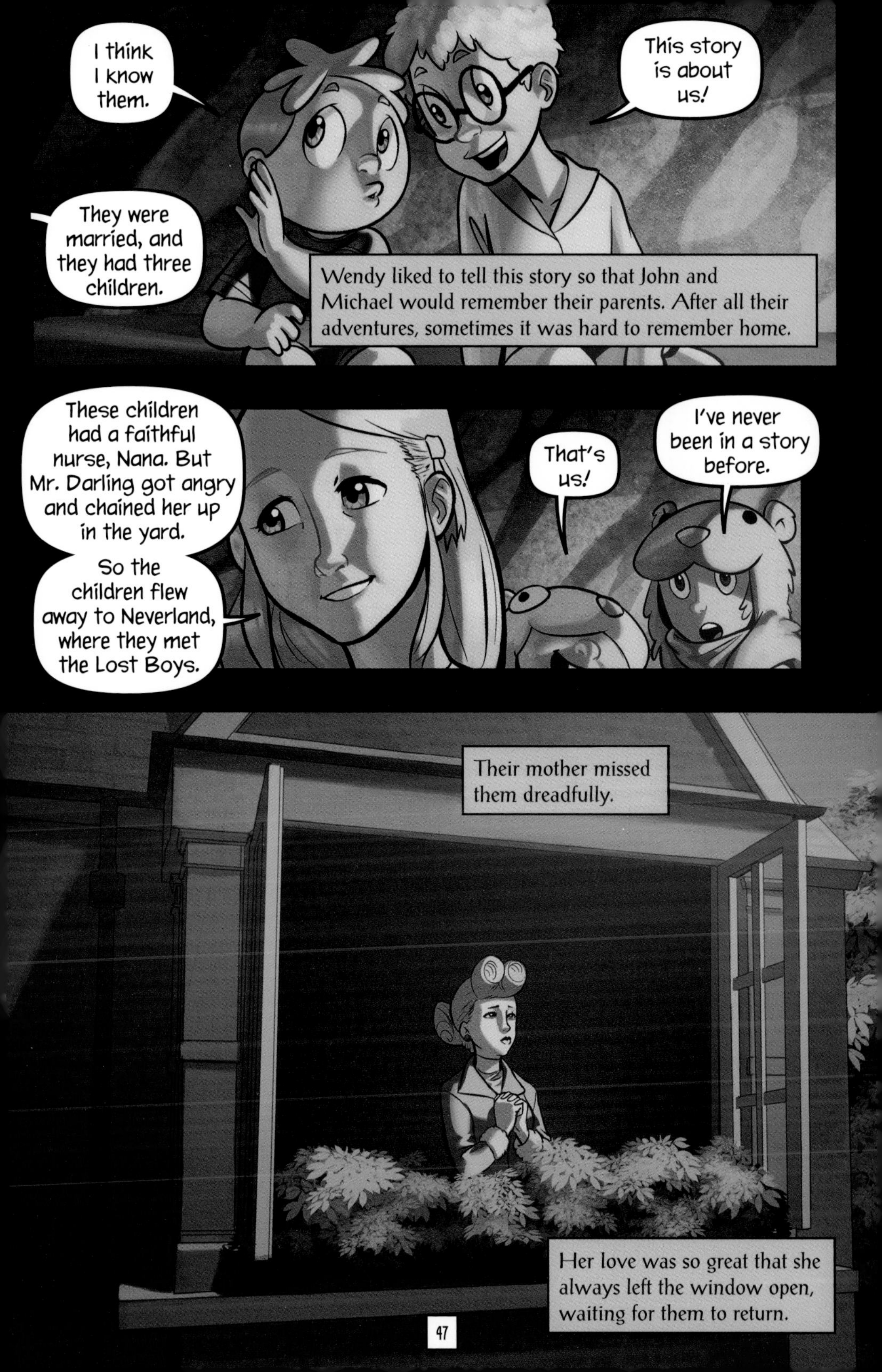
I think I know them.
This story is about us!
They were married, and they had three children.
Wendy liked to tell this story so that John and Michael would remember their parents. After all their adventures, sometimes it was hard to remember home.
These children had a faithful nurse, Nana. But Mr. Darling got angry and chained her up in the yard.
So the children flew away to Neverland, where they met the Lost Boys.
That's us!
I've never been in a story before.
Their mother missed them dreadfully.
Her love was so great that she always left the window open, waiting for them to return.

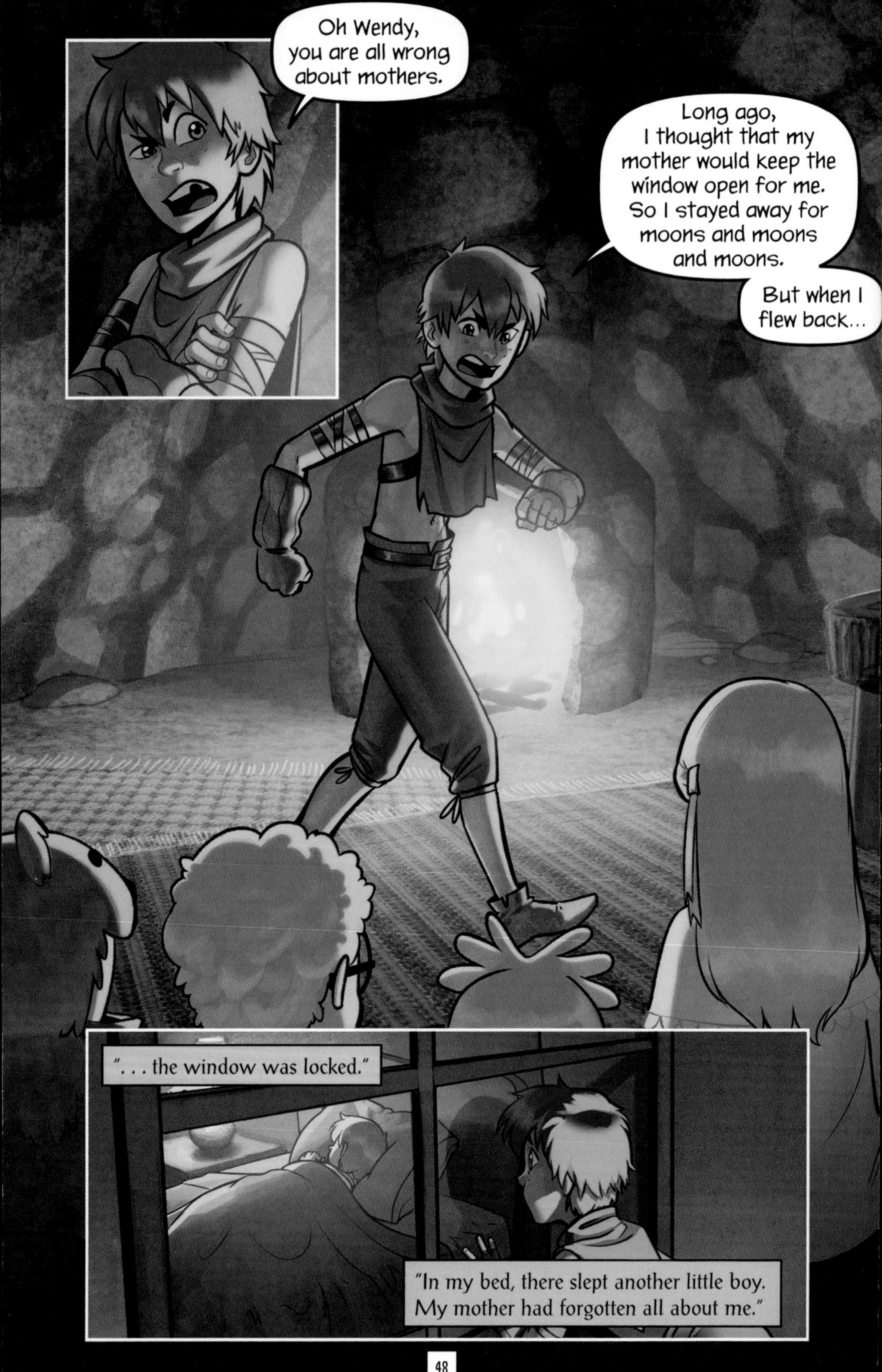

Oh Wendy, you are all wrong about mothers.
Long ago, I thought that my mother would keep the window open for me. So I stayed away for moons and moons and moons.
But when I flew back...
". . . the window was locked."
"In my bed, there slept another little boy. My mother had forgotten all about me."

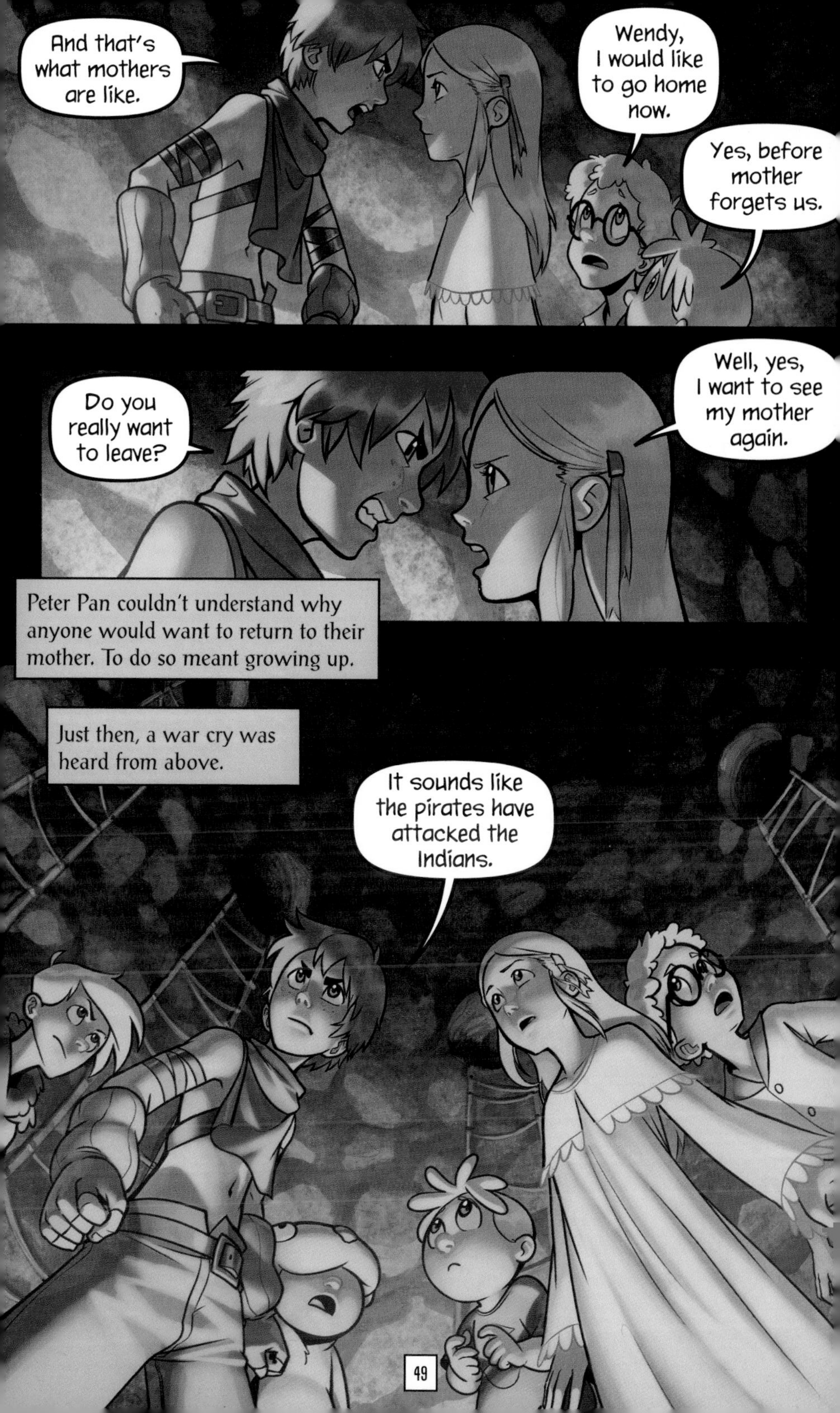
And that's what mothers are like.
Wendy, I would like to go home now.
Yes, before mother forgets us.
Do you really want to leave?
Well, yes, I want to see my mother again.
Peter Pan couldn't understand why anyone would want to return to their mother. To do so meant growing up.
Just then, a war cry was heard from above.
It sounds like the pirates have attacked the Indians.

CHAPTER 5
CAPTAIN HOOK

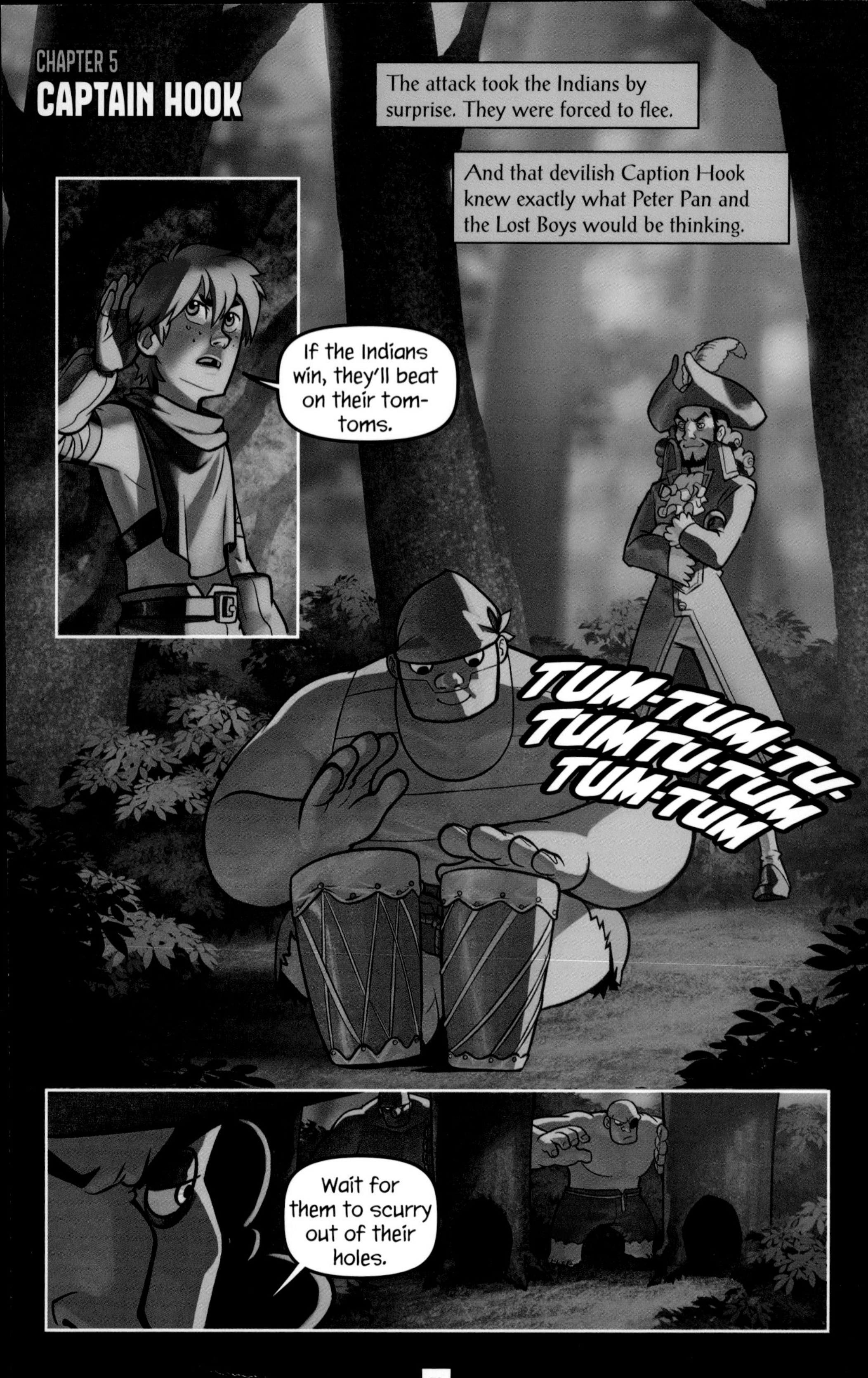
The attack took the Indians by surprise. They were forced to flee.
And that devilish Caption Hook knew exactly what Peter Pan and the Lost Boys would be thinking.
If the Indians win, they'll beat on their tom-toms.
TUM-TUM-TU-TUMTU-TUM TUM-TUM
Wait for them to scurry out of their holes.

An Indian victory!

Let's go see.

Go without me.

Umph!

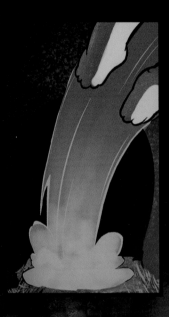

Uh-oh...

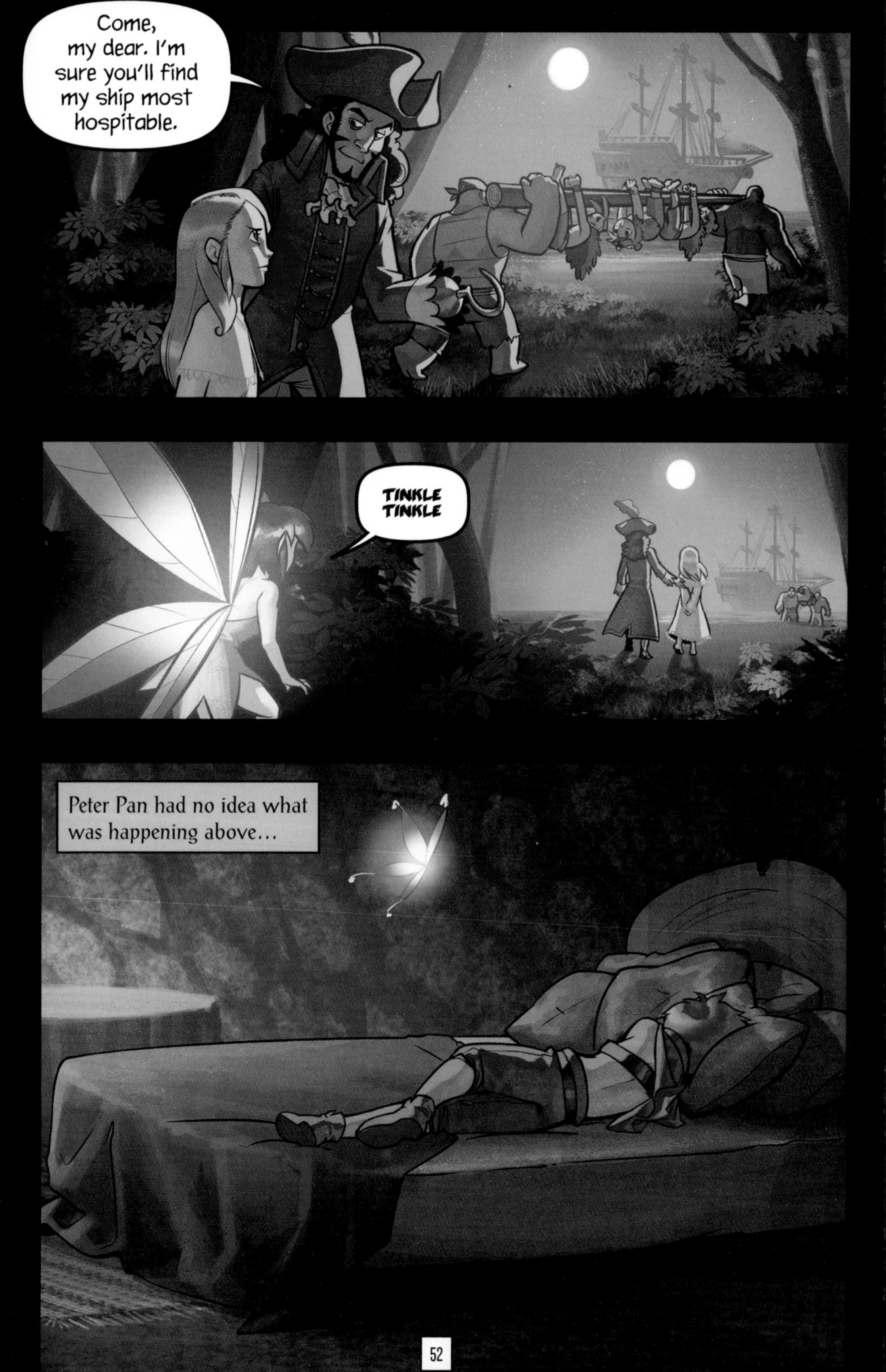
Come, my dear. I'm sure you'll find my ship most hospitable.
TINKLE TINKLE
Peter Pan had no idea what was happening above...

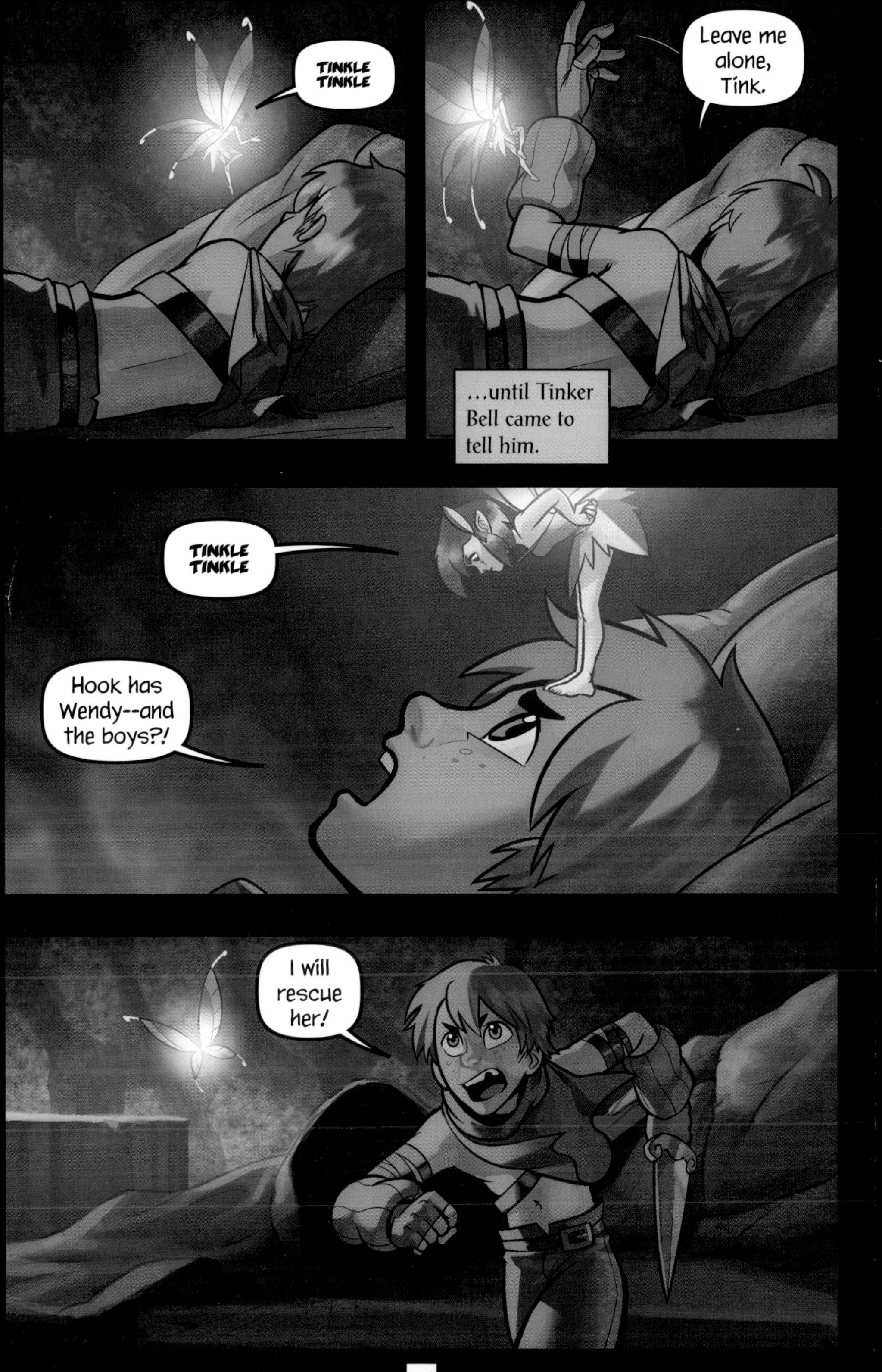
TINKLE TINKLE
Leave me alone, Tink.
...until Tinker Bell came to tell him.
TINKLE TINKLE
Hook has Wendy--and the boys?!
I will rescue her!

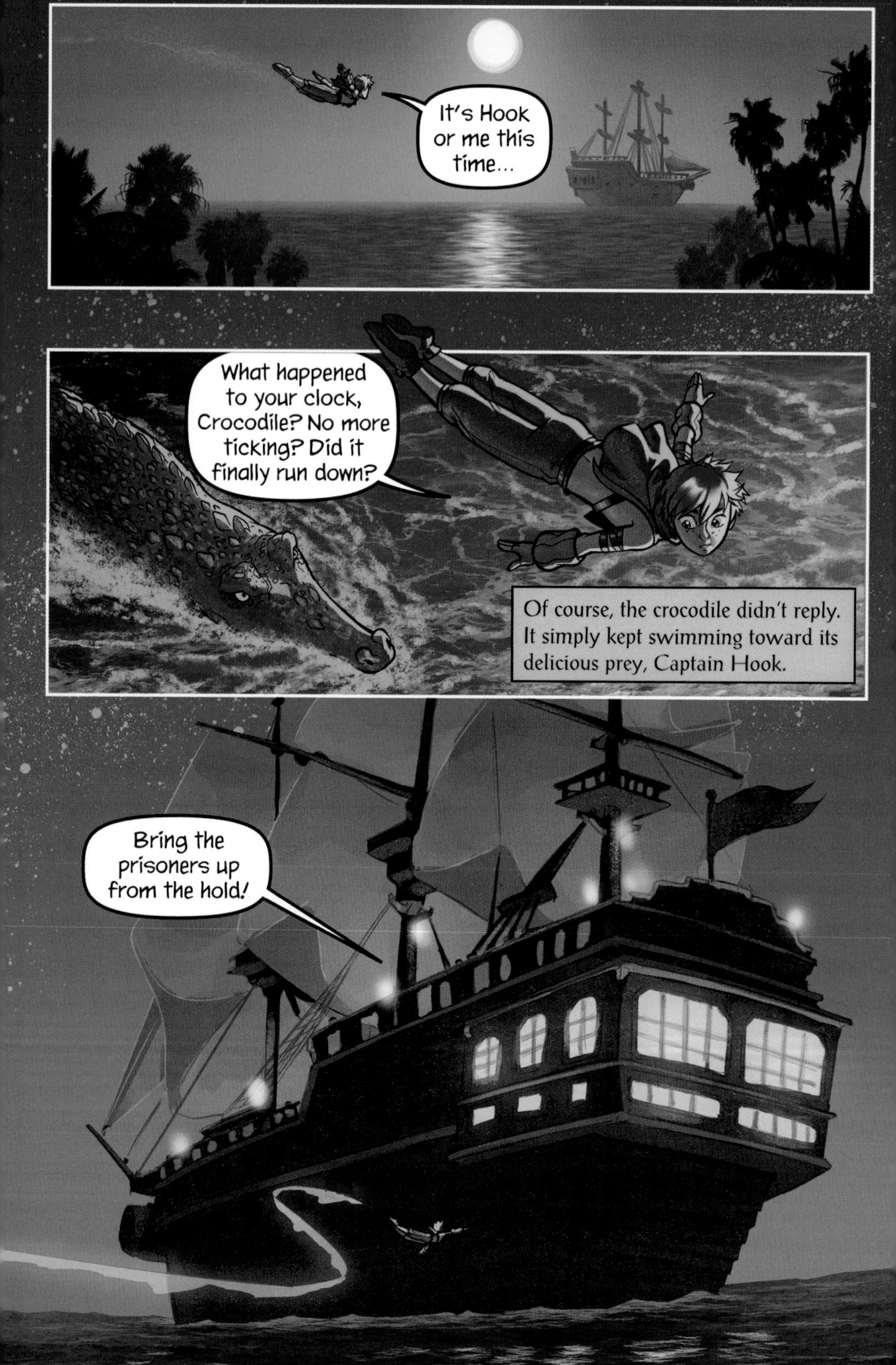
It's Hook or me this time...
What happened to your clock, Crocodile? No more ticking? Did it finally run down?
Of course, the crocodile didn't reply. It simply kept swimming toward its delicious prey, Captain Hook.
Bring the prisoners up from the hold!

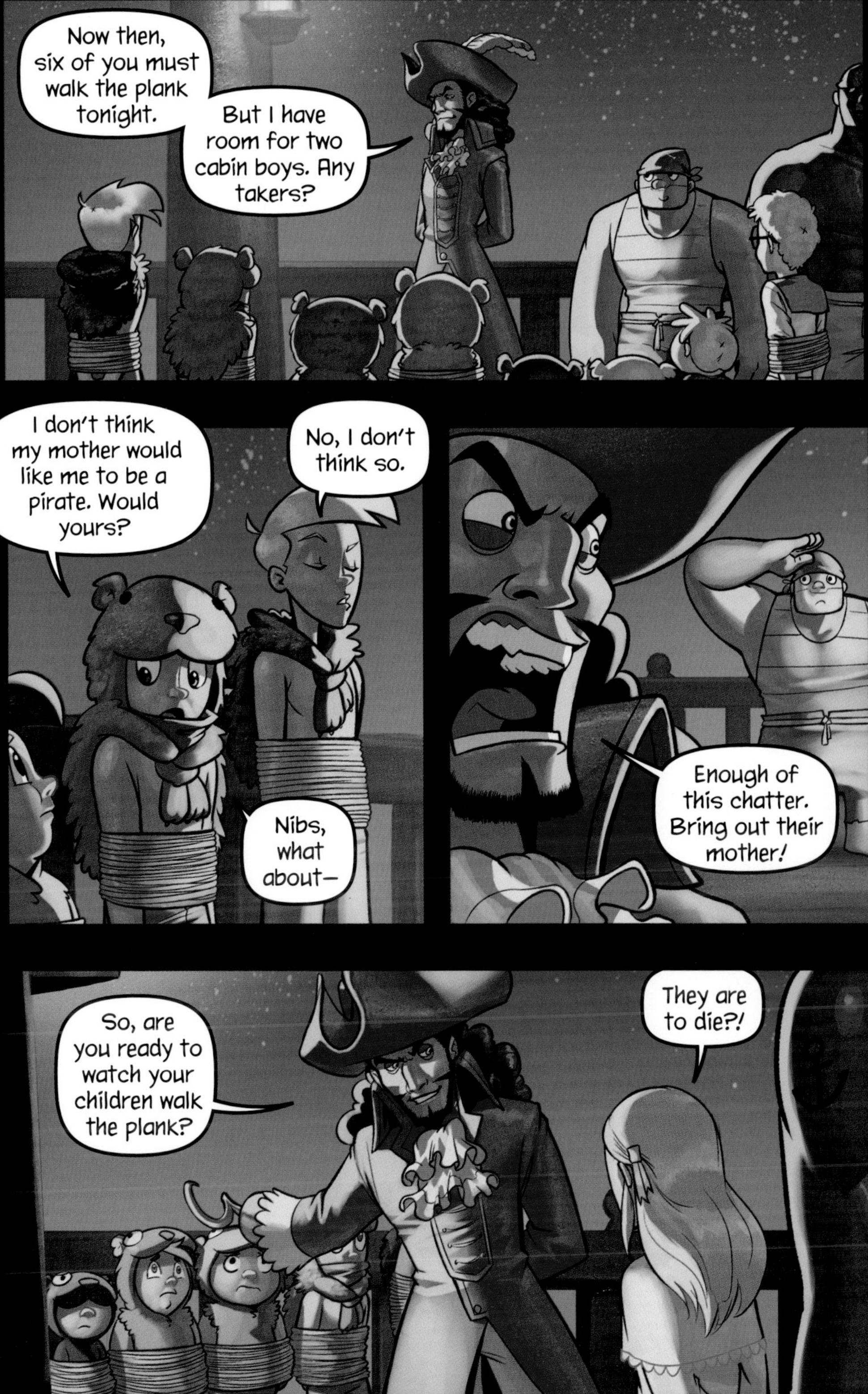
Now then, six of you must walk the plank tonight.
But I have room for two cabin boys. Any takers?
I don't think my mother would like me to be a pirate. Would yours?
No, I don't think so.
Nibs, what about—
Enough of this chatter. Bring out their mother!
So, are you ready to watch your children walk the plank?
They are to die?!

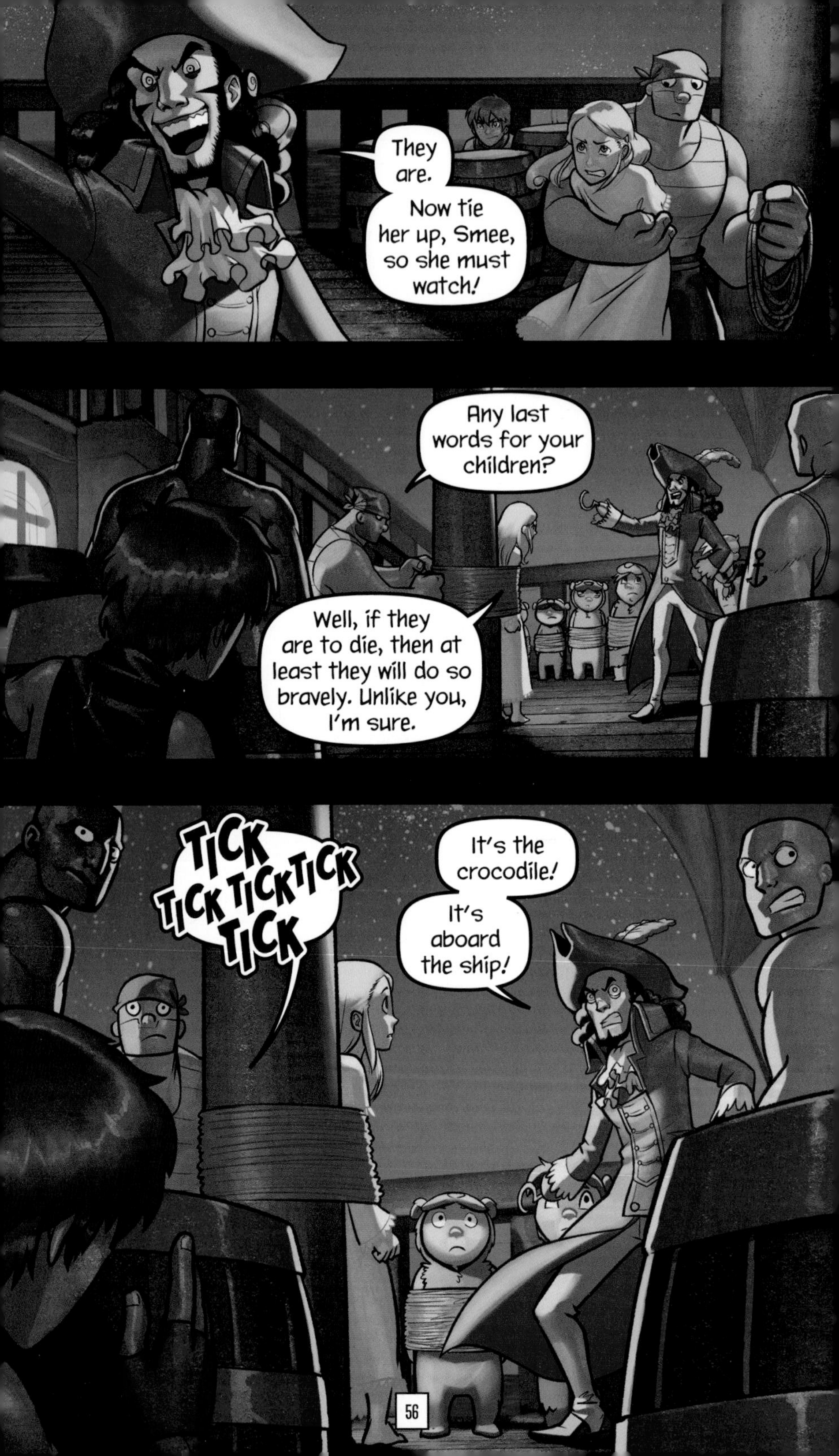
They are.
Now tie her up, Smee, so she must watch!
Any last words for your children?
Well, if they are to die, then at least they will do so bravely. Unlike you, I'm sure.
TICK TICK TICK TICK TICK
It's the crocodile!
It's aboard the ship!

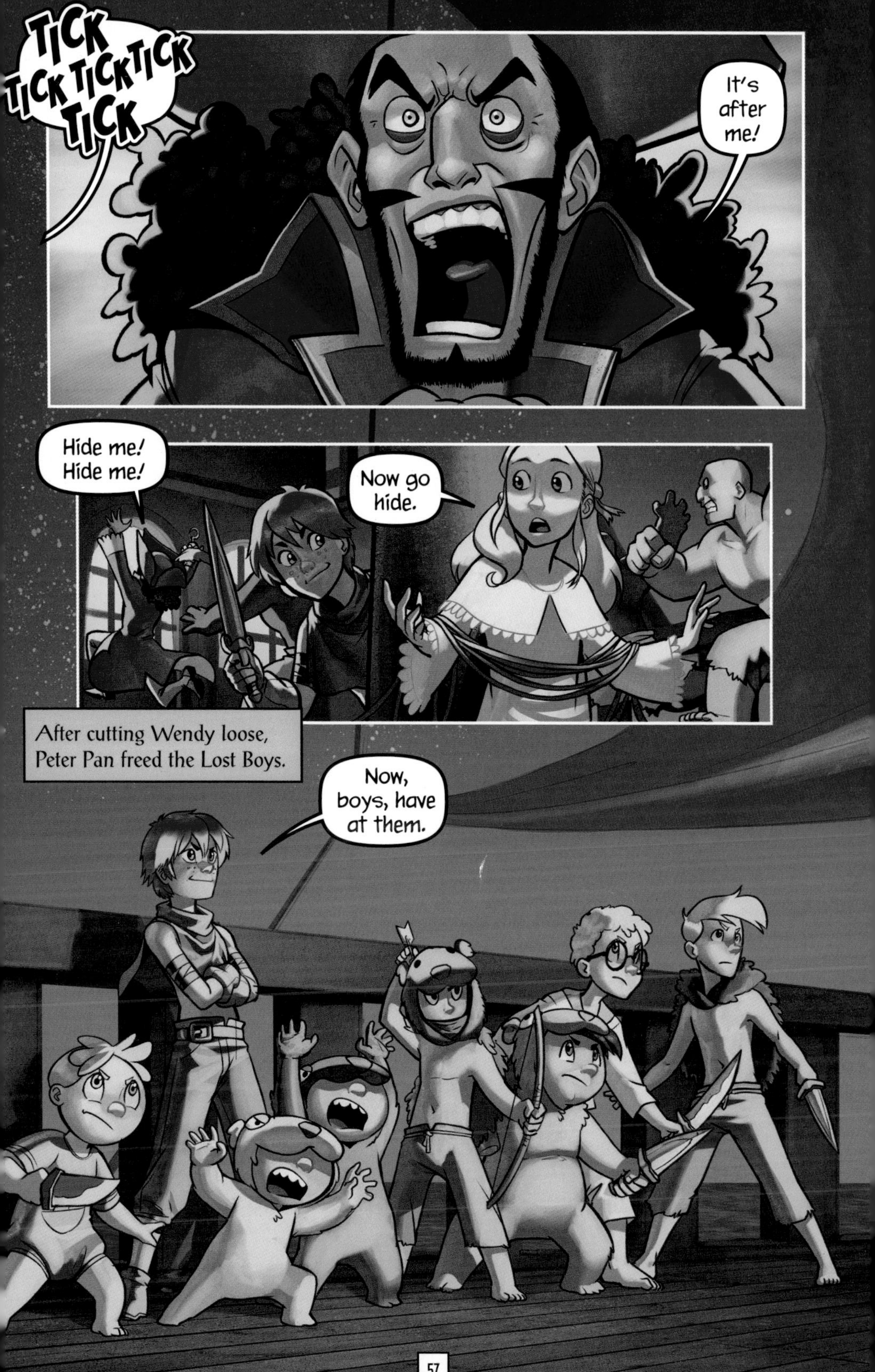
TICK TICK TICK TICK TICK TICK
It's after me!
Hide me! Hide me!
Now go hide.
After cutting Wendy loose, Peter Pan freed the Lost Boys.
Now, boys, have at them.

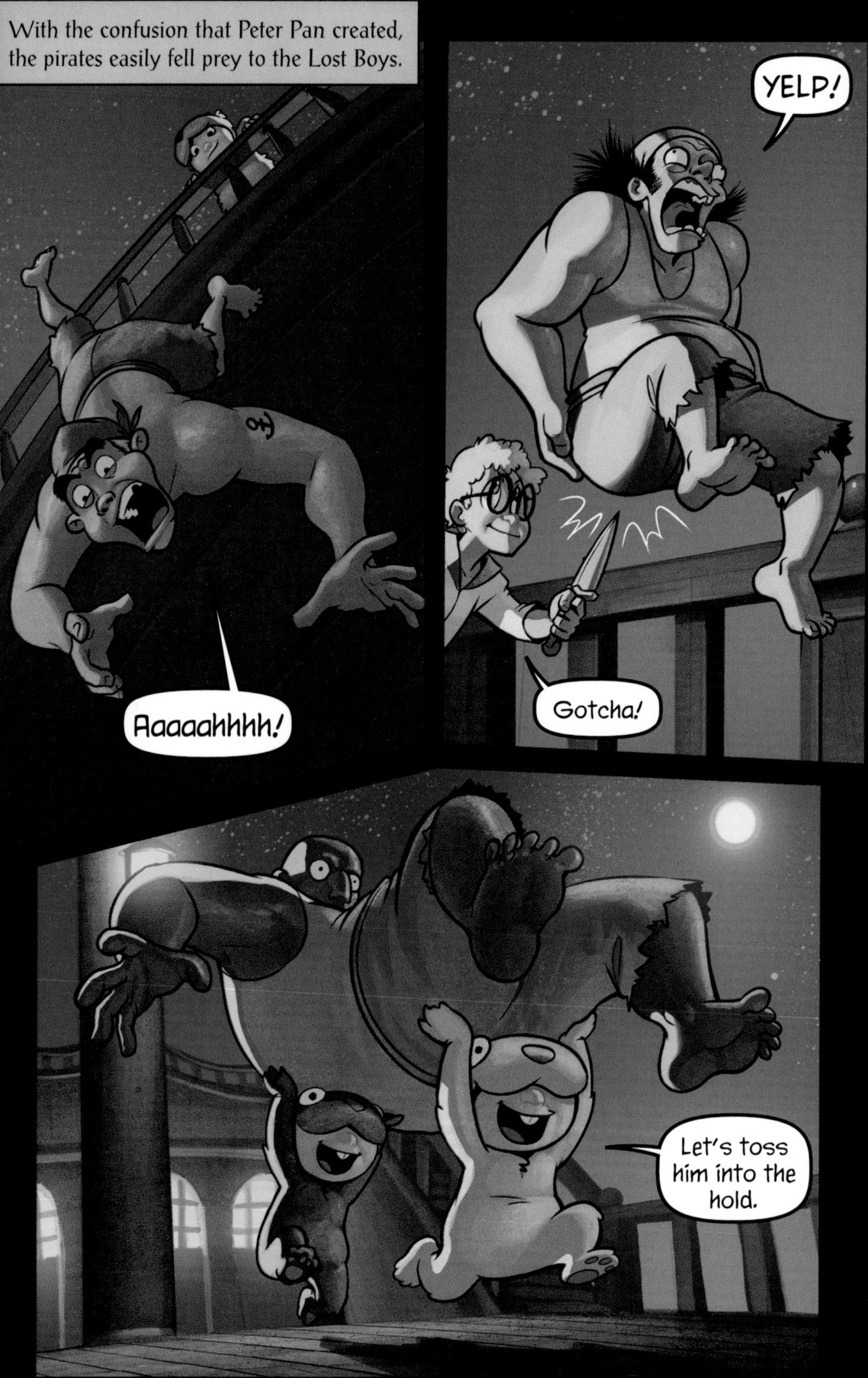
With the confusion that Peter Pan created, the pirates easily fell prey to the Lost Boys.
Aaaaahhhh!
YELP!
Gotcha!
Let's toss him into the hold.

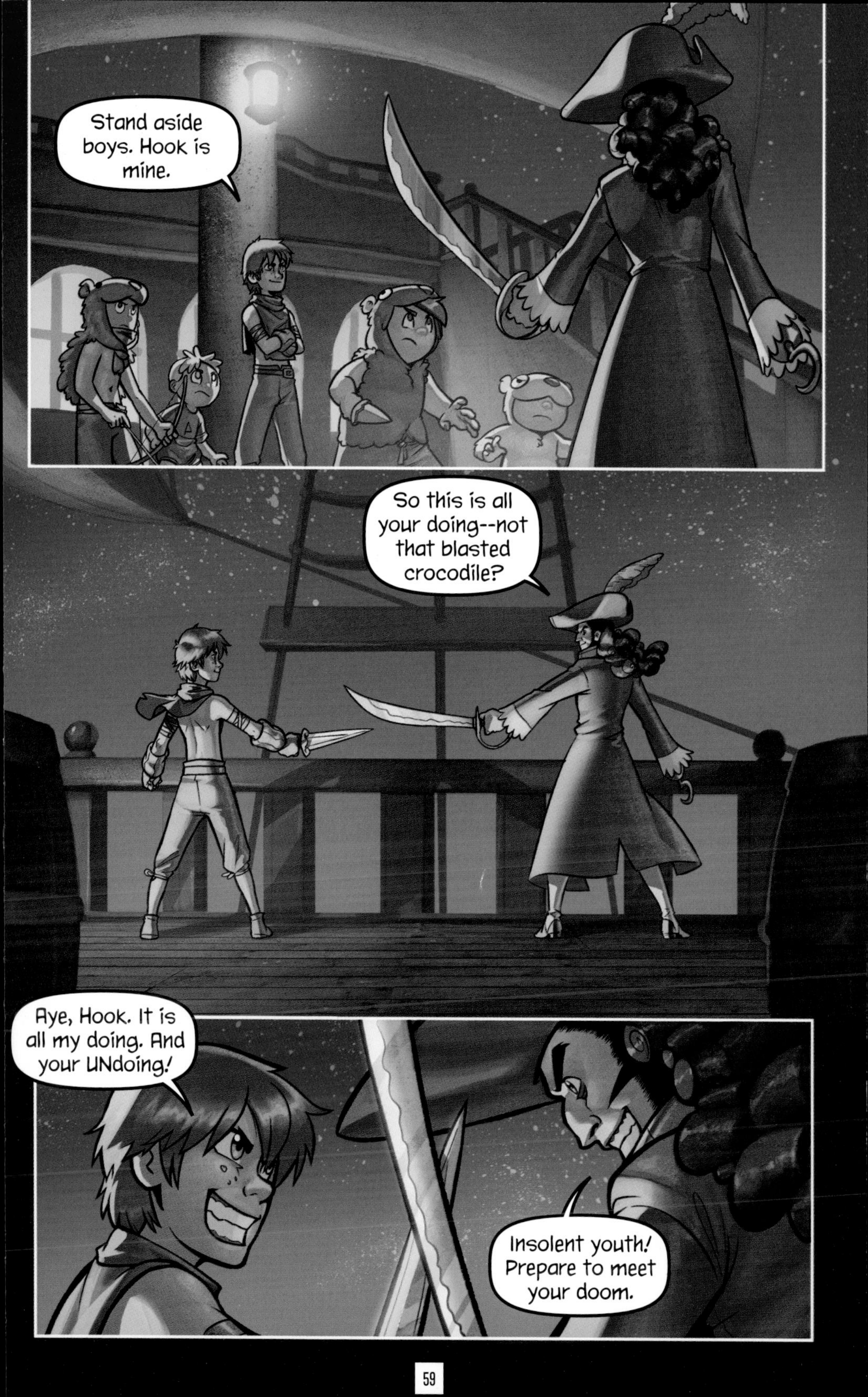
Stand aside boys. Hook is mine.
So this is all your doing--not that blasted crocodile?
Aye, Hook. It is all my doing. And your UNdoing!
Insolent youth! Prepare to meet your doom.

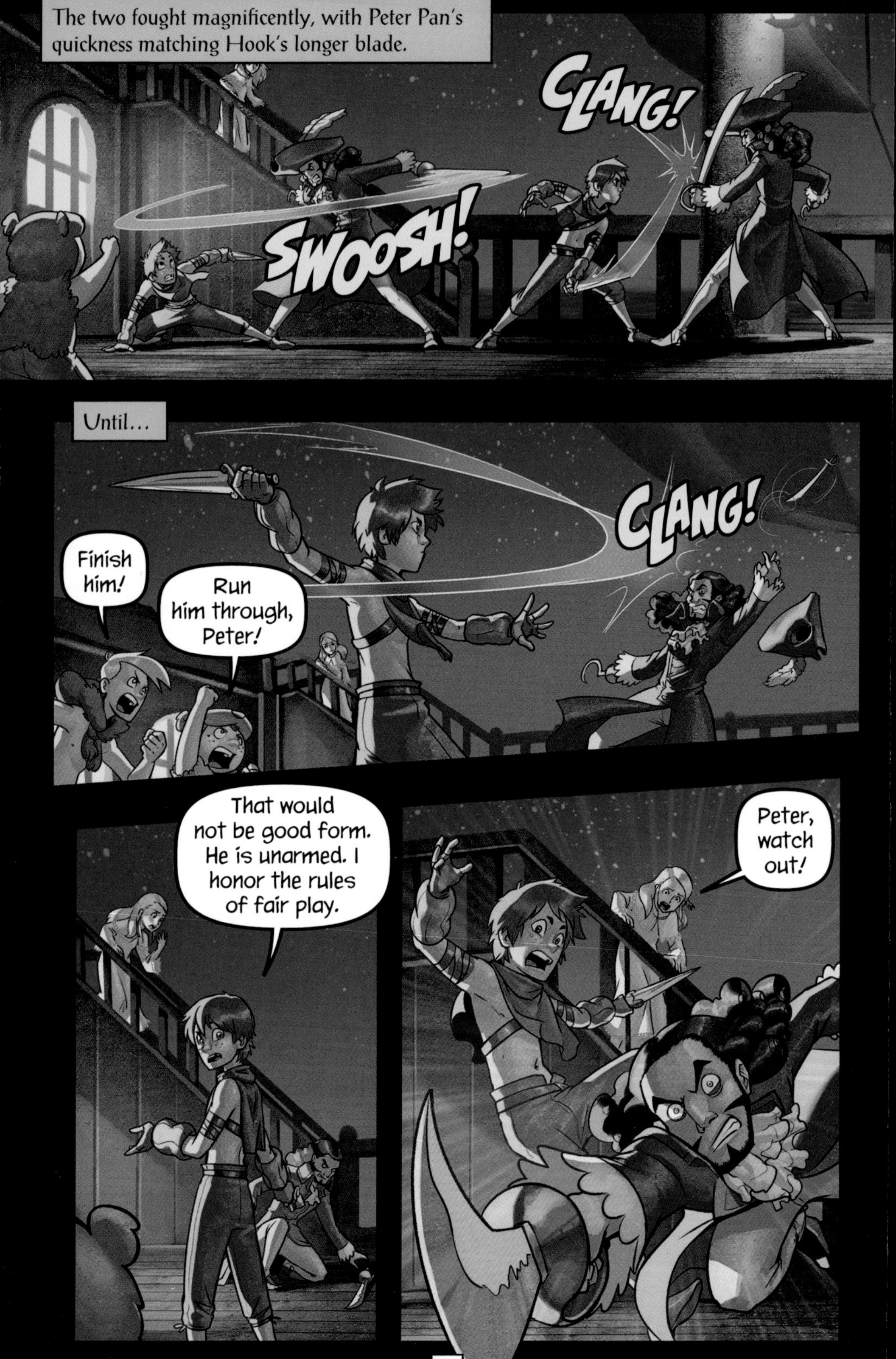
The two fought magnificently, with Peter Pan's quickness matching Hook's longer blade.
CLANG!
SWOOSH!
Until...
CLANG!
Finish him!
Run him through, Peter!
That would not be good form. He is unarmed. I honor the rules of fair play.
Peter, watch out!

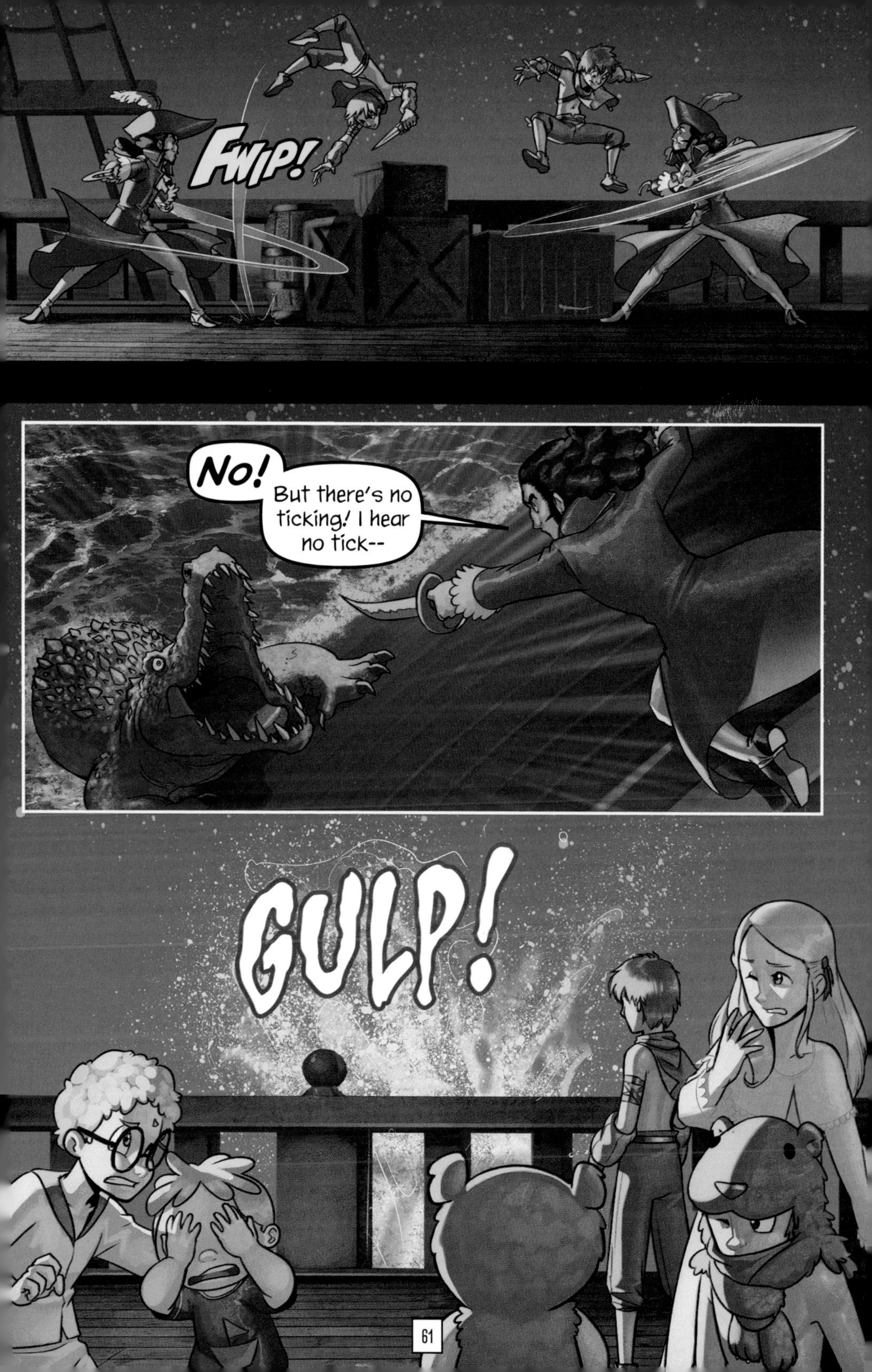
FWIP!
No!
But there's no ticking! I hear no tick--
GULP!

CHAPTER 6
THE RETURN HOME

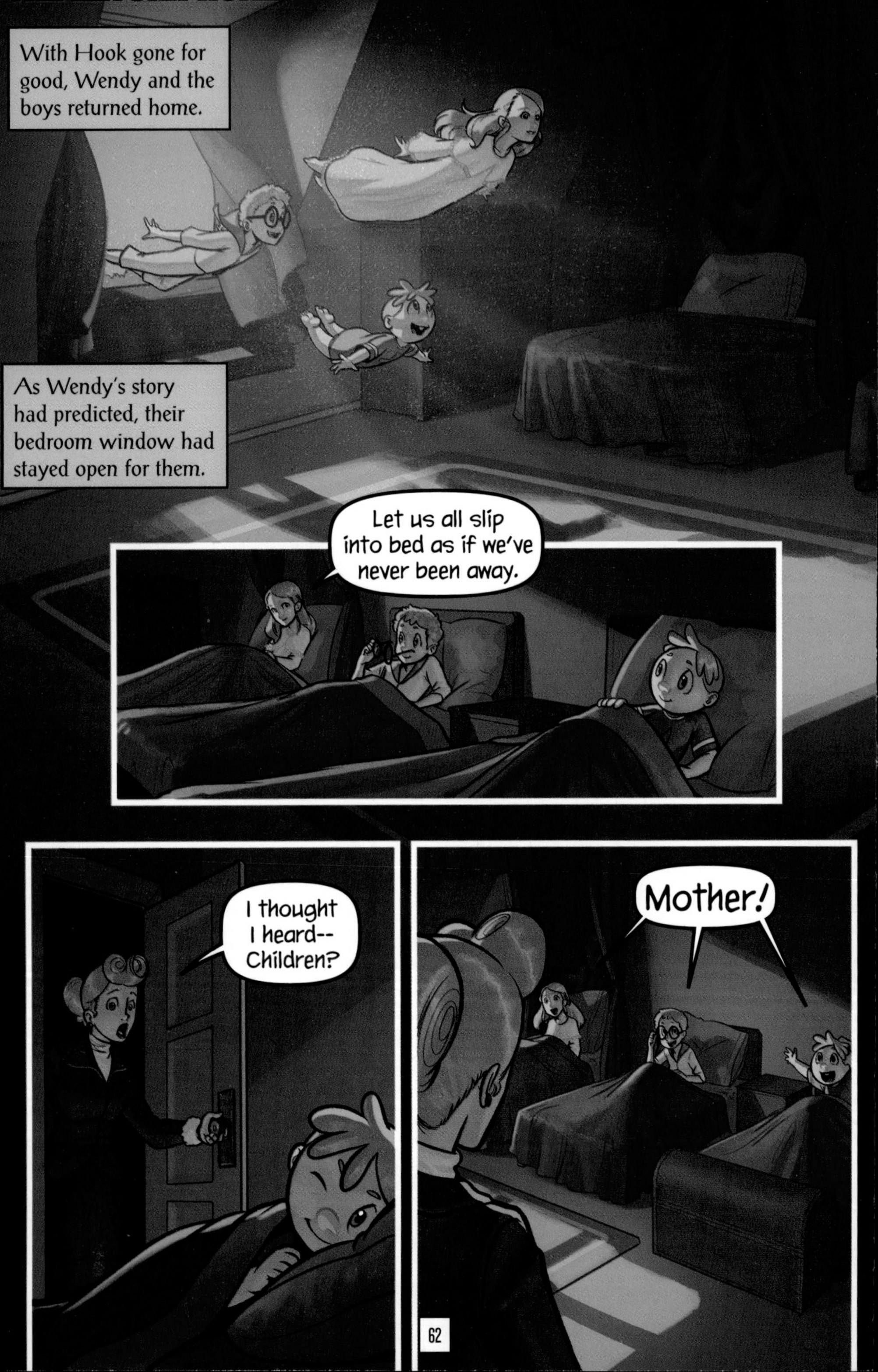

With Hook gone for good, Wendy and the boys returned home.
As Wendy's story had predicted, their bedroom window had stayed open for them.
Let us all slip into bed as if we've never been away.
I thought I heard-- Children?
Mother!

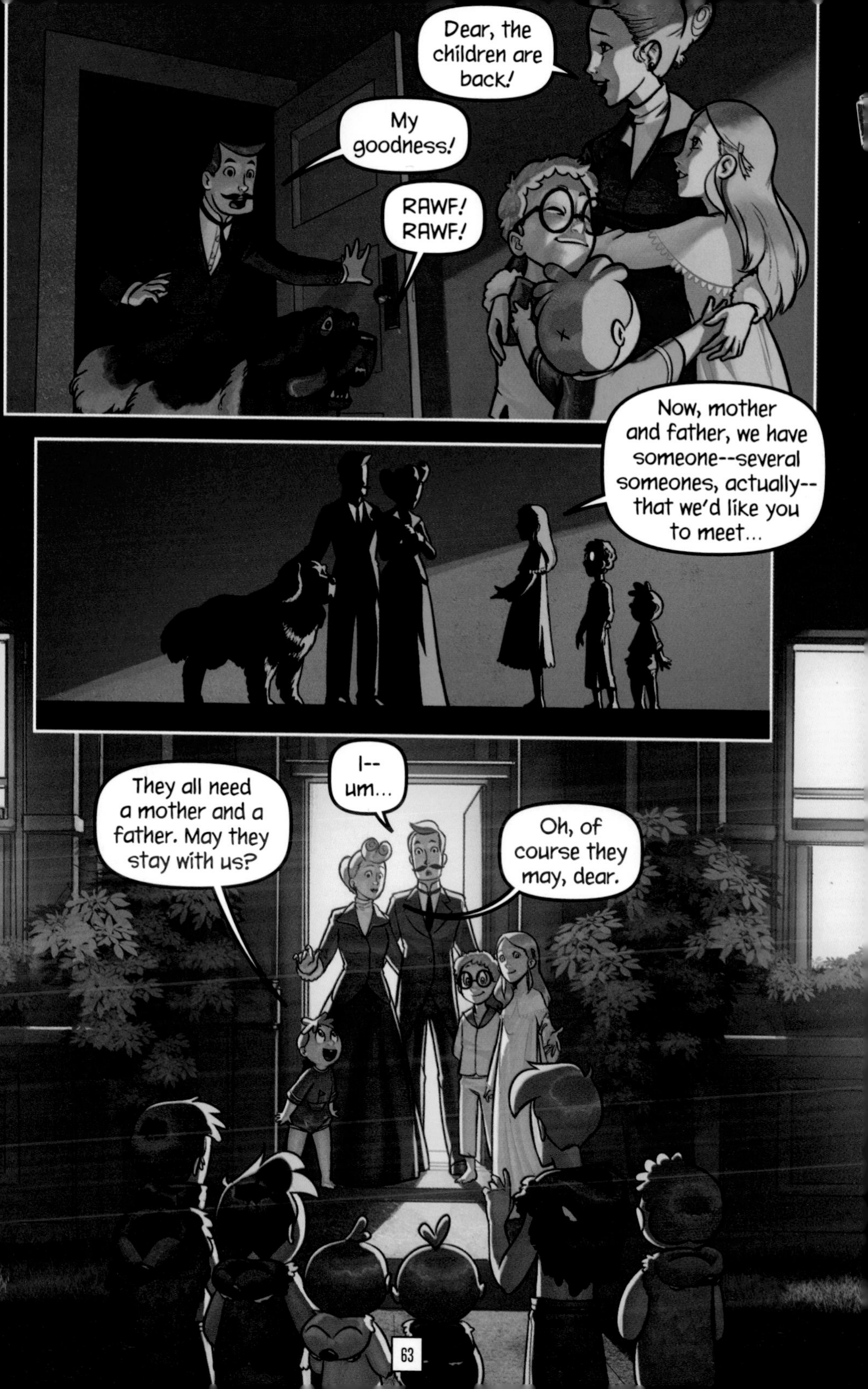
Dear, the children are back!
My goodness!
RAWF! RAWF!
Now, mother and father, we have someone--several someones, actually--that we'd like you to meet...
They all need a mother and a father. May they stay with us?
I-- um...
Oh, of course they may, dear.

Later, before bed, Peter Pan came to see Wendy before flying back to Neverland.

Will I ever see you again?

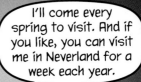

I'll come every spring to visit. And if you like, you can visit me in Neverland for a week each year.

Each year, for many years, Peter Pan came and took Wendy away for a week at a time.

But eventually he forgot to visit.

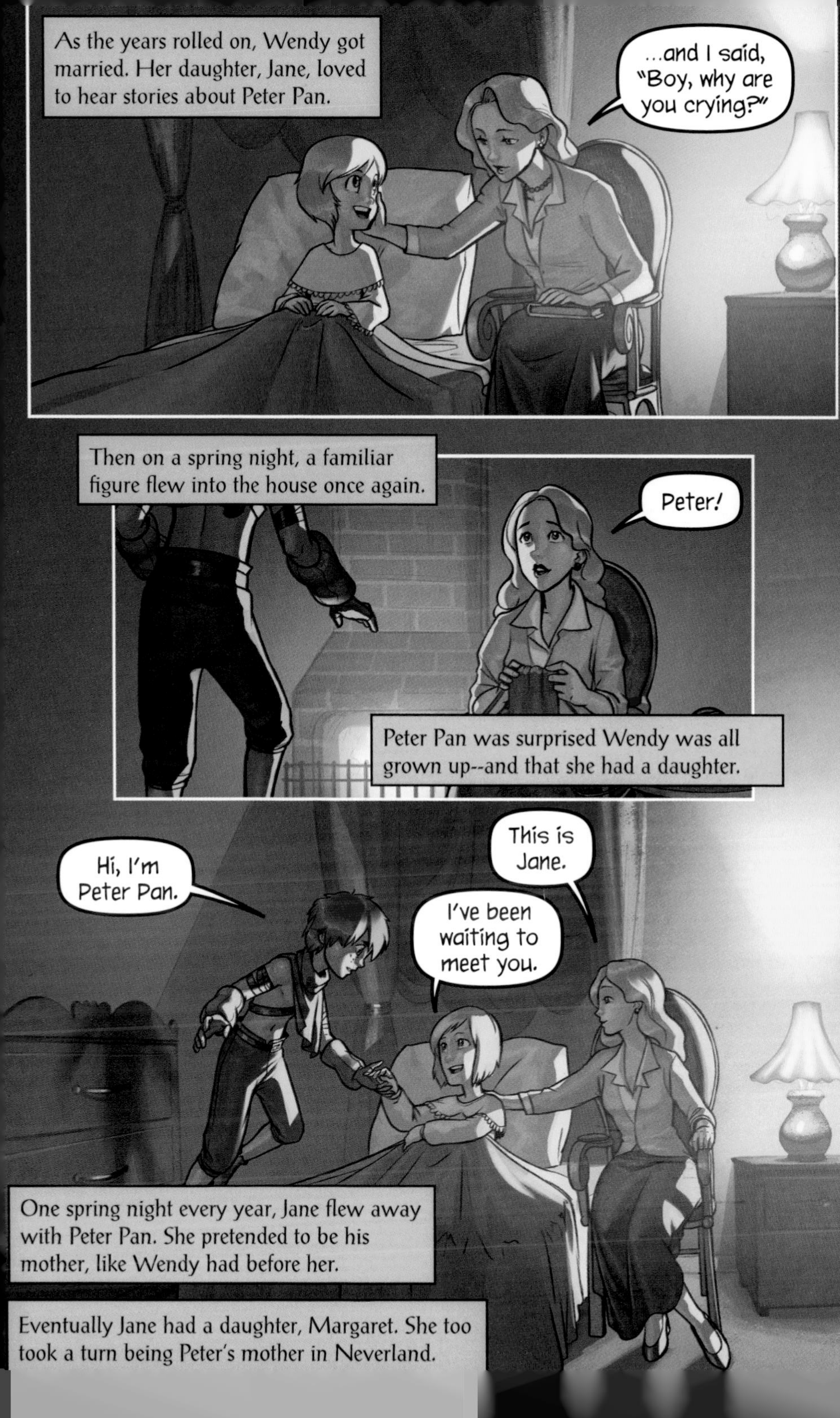
As the years rolled on, Wendy got married. Her daughter, Jane, loved to hear stories about Peter Pan.
...and I said, "Boy, why are you crying?"
Then on a spring night, a familiar figure flew into the house once again.
Peter!
Peter Pan was surprised Wendy was all grown up--and that she had a daughter.
Hi, I'm Peter Pan.
This is Jane.
I've been waiting to meet you.
One spring night every year, Jane flew away with Peter Pan. She pretended to be his mother, like Wendy had before her.
Eventually Jane had a daughter, Margaret. She too took a turn being Peter's mother in Neverland.

ABOUT THE RETELLING AUTHOR AND ILLUSTRATOR

Blake Hoena grew up in central Wisconsin, where he wrote stories about robots conquering the moon and trolls lumbering around the woods behind his parents house. He now lives in St. Paul, Minnesota, with his wife, two kids, a dog, and a couple of cats. Blake continues to make up stories about things like space aliens and superheroes, and he has written more than 70 chapter books and graphic novels for children.

Fernando Cano is an emerging illustrator born in Mexico City, Mexico. He currently resides in Monterrey, Mexico. He has done illustration work for Marvel, DC Comics, Stone Arch Books, and role-playing games from Paizo Publishing. In his spare time, he enjoys hanging out with friends, singing, rowing, and drawing.

GLOSSARY

crept (KREPT)—moved slowly with the body close to the ground

cunning (KUNN-ing)—cleverness or skill, especially at tricking people to get what you want

flickering (FLIK-er-ing)—quick and unsteady moving of light, like turning a light switch off and on rapidly

jealous (JELL-uhss)—feeling or showing an unhappy or angry desire to have what someone else has

lagoon (luh-GOON)—an area of sea water that is separated from the ocean by a reef or sandbar

modest (MAH-desst)—not very large in size or amount

nurse (NERSS)—an old-fashioned term for a woman who is paid to take care of a young child in the child's home

pursued (per-SOOD)—followed and tried to catch or capture

ruin (ROON)—damage or spoil

stalked (STALKT)—followed stealthily and sneakily

COMMON CORE ALIGNED
READING QUESTIONS

1. **Why does Peter Pan return to the Darling children's bedroom as they are trying to fall asleep?** *("Read closely to determine what the text says explicitly and to make logical inferences from it; cite specific textual evidence when writing or speaking to support conclusions drawn from the text.")*

2. **Who is Captain Hook, and why is he so important to the story? What is his relationship with Peter?** *("Analyze the structure of texts, including how specific sentences, paragraphs, and larger portions of the text (e.g., a section, chapter, scene, or stanza) relate to each other and the whole.")*

3. **Why do Peter and the Lost Boys want to remain children forever? Would you want to remain a child forever? Why or why not?** *("Analyze how and why individuals, events, and ideas develop and interact over the course of a text.")*

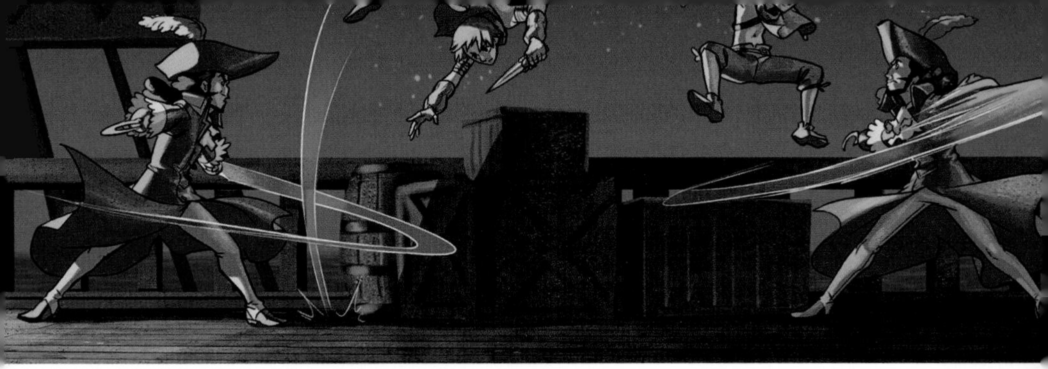

COMMON CORE ALIGNED
WRITING PROMPTS

1. **Imagine that you were one of the Darling children and you had your journal in one your pajama pocket on your adventures. What would you include in your journal about Neverland? Write about it!** *("Write informative/explanatory texts to examine and convey complex ideas and information clearly and accurately through the effective selection, organization, and analysis of content.")*

2. **Pretend you are Captain Hook. Write a letter to a future reader of this story explaining his point of view concerning Peter Pan and the Lost Boys.** *("Produce clear and coherent writing in which the development, organization, and style are appropriate to task, purpose, and audience.")*

3. **First describe your favorite setting in the story (feel free to look back into the story for good ideas). Once you've done that, write an essay that explains why this is your favorite setting.** *("Produce clear and coherent writing in which the development, organization, and style are appropriate to task, purpose, and audience.")*

READ THEM ALL!

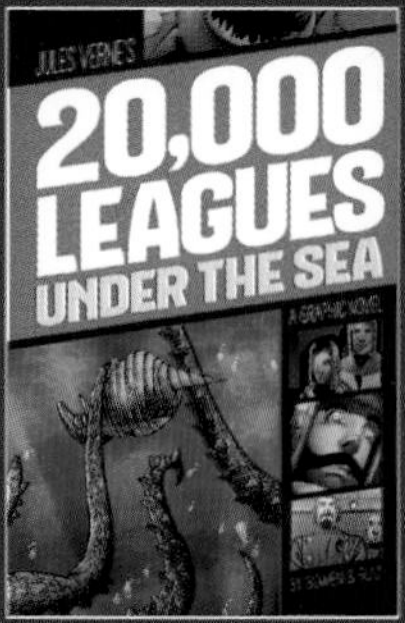
JULES VERNE'S
20,000 LEAGUES UNDER THE SEA
A GRAPHIC NOVEL

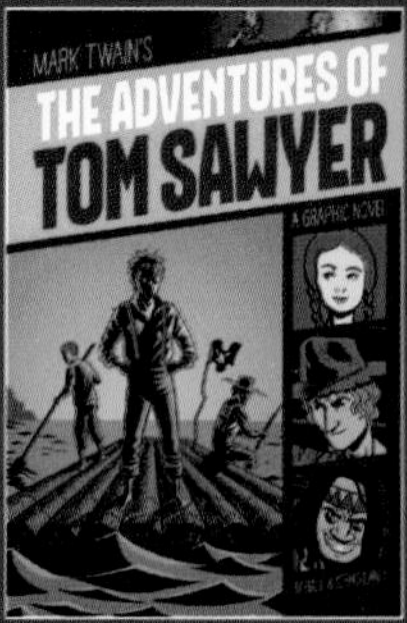
MARK TWAIN'S
THE ADVENTURES OF TOM SAWYER
A GRAPHIC NOVEL

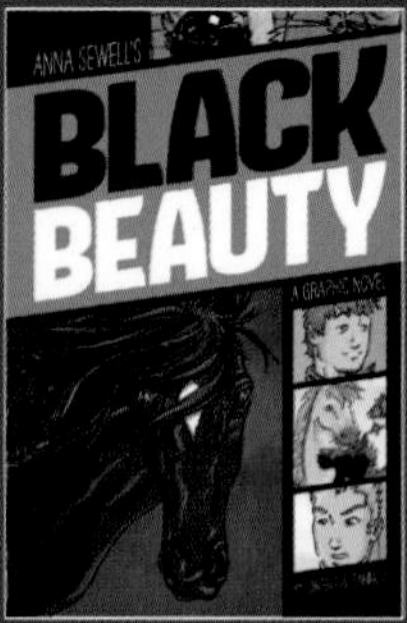
ANNA SEWELL'S
BLACK BEAUTY
A GRAPHIC NOVEL

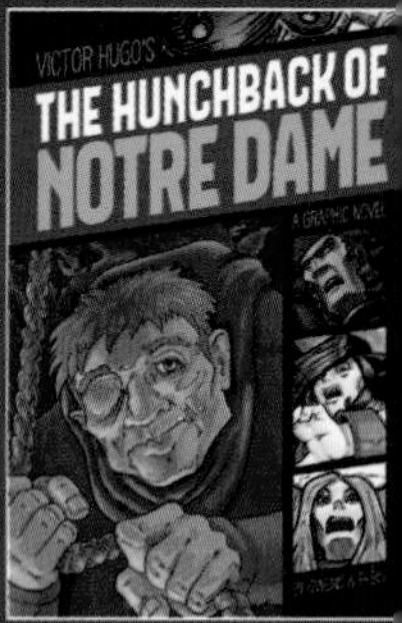
VICTOR HUGO'S
THE HUNCHBACK OF NOTRE DAME
A GRAPHIC NOVEL

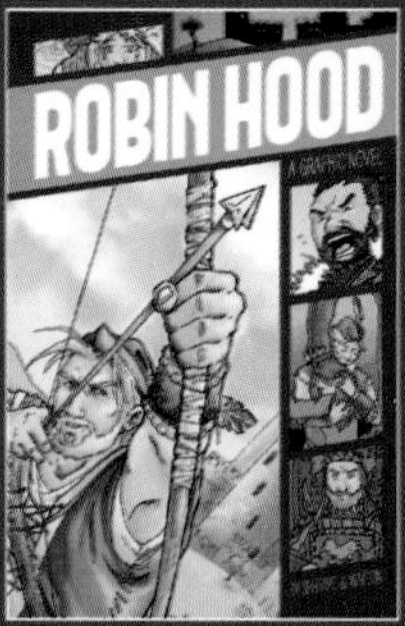
ROBIN HOOD
A GRAPHIC NOVEL

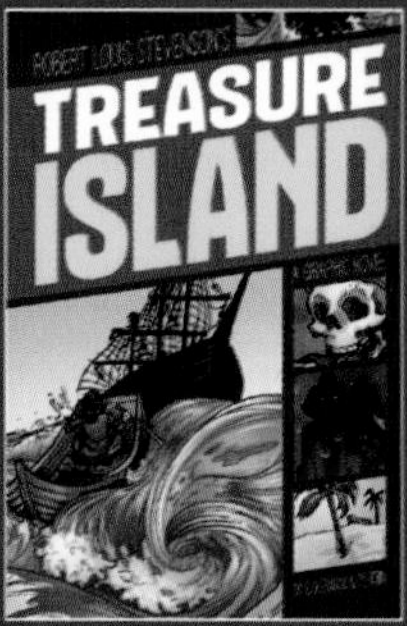
ROBERT LOUIS STEVENSON'S
TREASURE ISLAND
A GRAPHIC NOVEL

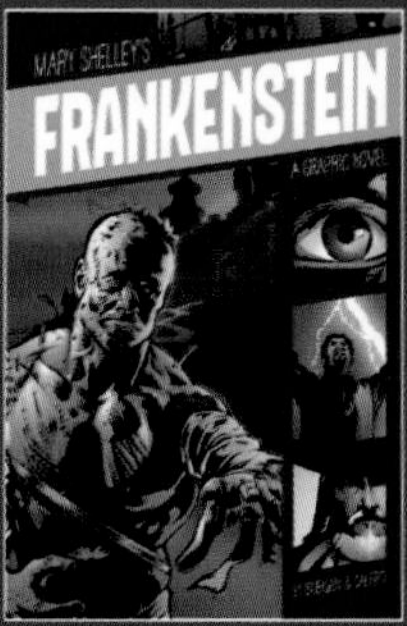
MARY SHELLEY'S
FRANKENSTEIN
A GRAPHIC NOVEL

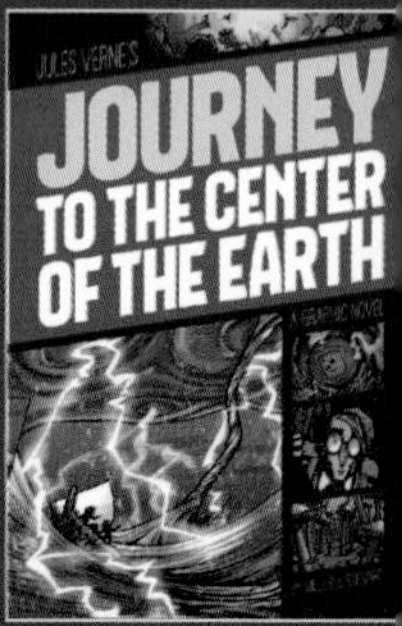
JULES VERNE'S
JOURNEY TO THE CENTER OF THE EARTH
A GRAPHIC NOVEL

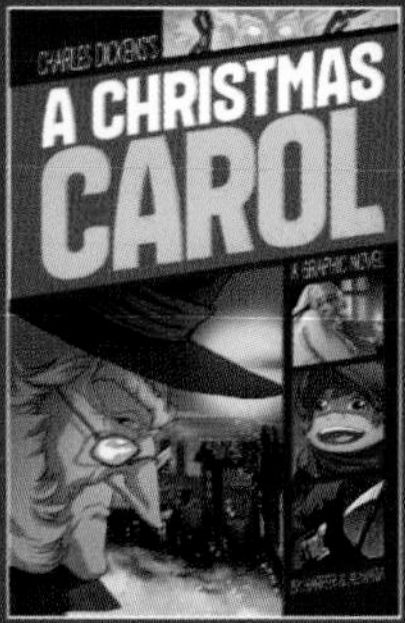
CHARLES DICKENS'S
A CHRISTMAS CAROL
A GRAPHIC NOVEL

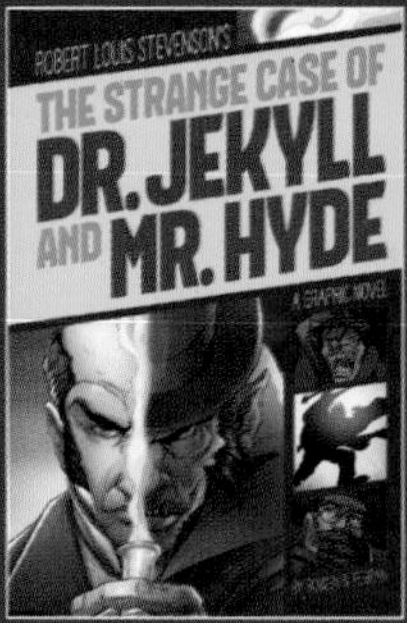
ROBERT LOUIS STEVENSON'S
THE STRANGE CASE OF DR. JEKYLL AND MR. HYDE
A GRAPHIC NOVEL

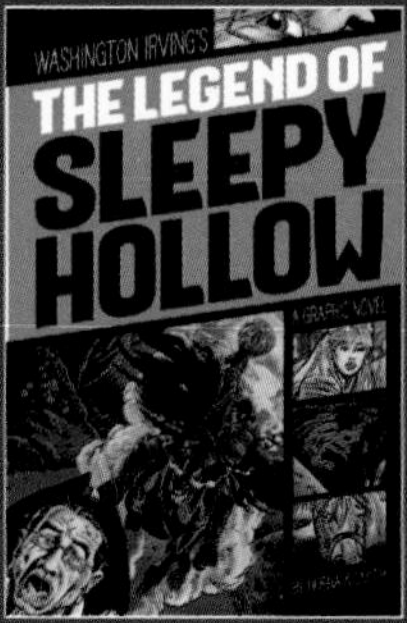
WASHINGTON IRVING'S
THE LEGEND OF SLEEPY HOLLOW
A GRAPHIC NOVEL

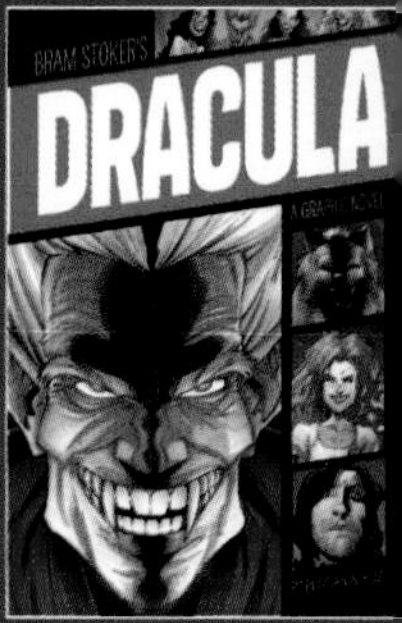
BRAM STOKER'S
DRACULA

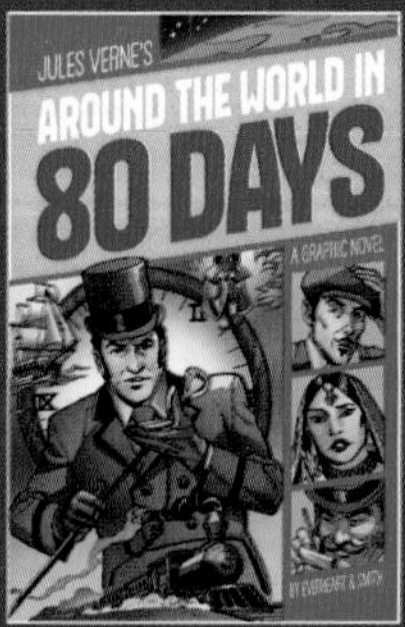
JULES VERNE'S
AROUND THE WORLD IN 80 DAYS
A GRAPHIC NOVEL

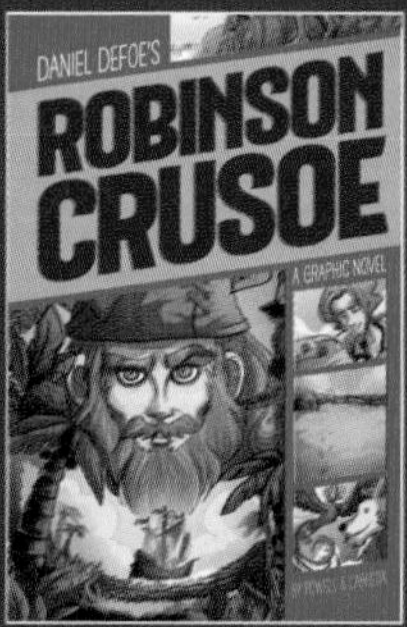
DANIEL DEFOE'S
ROBINSON CRUSOE
A GRAPHIC NOVEL

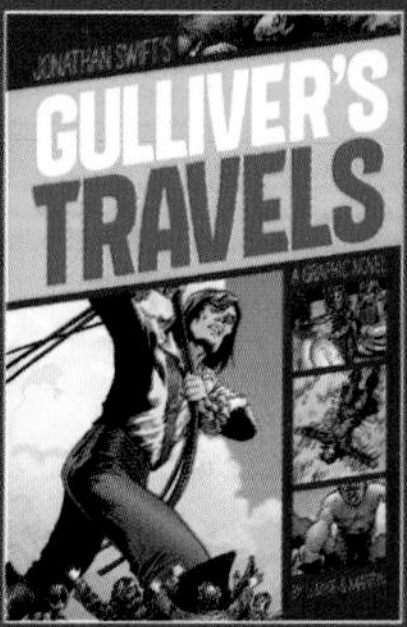
JONATHAN SWIFT'S
GULLIVER'S TRAVELS
A GRAPHIC NOVEL

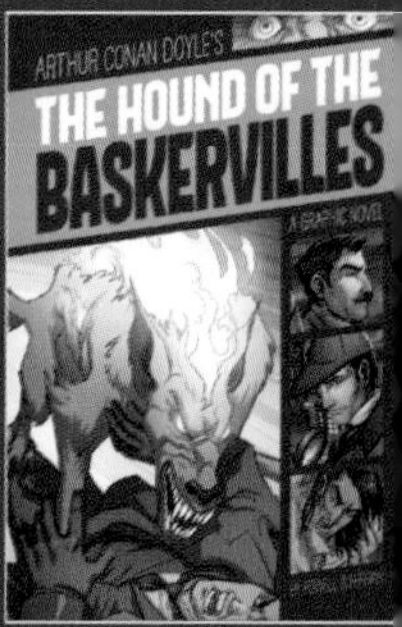
ARTHUR CONAN DOYLE'S
THE HOUND OF THE BASKERVILLES
A GRAPHIC NOVEL

JOHANN DAVID WYSS

THE SWISS FAMILY ROBINSON

A GRAPHIC NOVEL

PERSEUS AND MEDUSA

A GRAPHIC NOVEL

LEWIS CARROLL'S

ALICE IN WONDERLAND

A GRAPHIC NOVEL

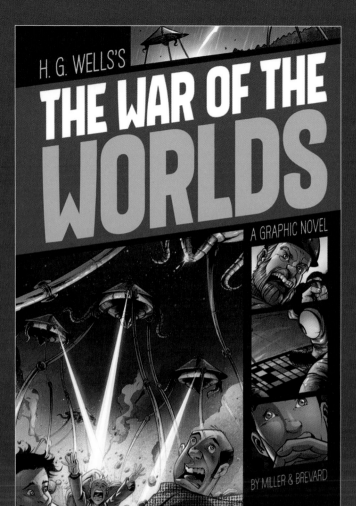

H. G. WELLS'S

THE WAR OF THE WORLDS

A GRAPHIC NOVEL

BY MILLER & BREVARD

H.G. WELLS'S

THE TIME MACHINE

A GRAPHIC NOVEL

BY DAVIS & RUIZ

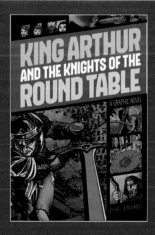

KING ARTHUR AND THE KNIGHTS OF THE ROUND TABLE

A GRAPHIC NOVEL

BY HALL & RICHARDS

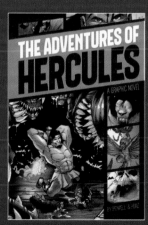

THE ADVENTURES OF HERCULES

A GRAPHIC NOVEL

BY BENTELL & RUIZ

ONLY FROM STONE ARCH BOOKS!